REVIEWS

Drop a pebble in the water: just a splash and it is gone;
But there's half-a-hundred ripples circling on and on and on.

These are words found in James Foley's famous poem, *Drop a Pebble*, and part of which is repeated at the conclusion of Robert Thornhill's 12th novel of the Walt Williams Mystery/Crime series, *Lady Justice and the Class Reunion.*

Thornhill masterly interweaves Walt's job as a policeman with the KCPD and his 50 year high school class reunion into a tale which includes three seniors who are friends now residing in a senior living center who come into possession of dangerous information about a Mexican drug cartel which has set up shop in KC; the problem of student bullying and a resultant weapons incident at Walt's alma mater; and the stalking and a subsequent shooting of a person at the local dinner/theater involving two former classmates...all told with exciting chases and moments of Thornhill's humor.

Even Elvis makes a re-appearance in solving one of the cases.

When the dust settles and the bad guys have been eliminated, Walt's lesson from Pastor Bob is that we all makes splashes in the water with decisions we make in our lives, and that these splashes create ripples effecting others and their subsequent decisions, and on and on. It is good when these ripples, even if they are personally painful, help Lady Justice restore balance to our world.

I found this book to have just the right balance of action, topical subject matter, and humor!

Christina Jones, Independence, MO.

****

Lady Justice and the Class Reunion is another great addition to the Lady Justice series. Once again we follow Walt and Ox as they investigate a series of robberies at a local gym, track down a merciless drug lord who has taken residence in their town and catch a stalker who has been holding a torch for one of his fellow classmates.

As always, Walt finds himself in situations that you cannot imagine. In the latest installment, he takes on a bull, a drug lord and learns how to play Mario Kart with his longtime tenant Jerry. There is never a dull moment in Walt's world. This time he and Ox receive help from an unlikely trio who believe that it is their duty to bring down the drug dealer who is enticing young women to become drug mules. Without their help, the police department would have no leads and still be at square one in their investigation.

If you are a fan of the Lady Justice series, you will not be disappointed with the latest installment. All of the characters that we have come to love are back. Walt even convinces Mary to participate in an aerobics class! If you are new to the series, the well-written characters and all of the unbelievable antics that Walt gets into will draw you in. This is a great series and I highly recommend it to everyone. Michelle Castillo, Article WriteUp

****

A priest hears a confession regarding drug smugglers. The drug cartel is using young women to smuggle drugs, and how they do it can cause the death of the young drug runners. Wanting to help these people get caught, yet wanting to keep his vows as a priest, the Padre and two of his friends decide to put out some hints in the hopes the police will figure it out. Walt and gang are hot on the case. Will they get to catch the criminals before more young women turn up missing and dead?

Add to this, it is Walt's 50th High School Reunion, and he is dragged into the planning committee. The plot thickens as a man ends up shot and it appears one of his classmates could be the main suspect.

Filled with laugh-out-loud moments, all the lovable characters are back and put in some hilarious situations. A fast paced fun read that will leave a smile on your face making you want more of Walt & The Gang. Sheri Wilkinson, Princeton, IL.

What Readers Are Saying

About The Lady Justice Series

This book is laugh-out-loud funny, on par with today's most popular writers! It's great see that old age and wisdom triumph over youth and exuberance again. Walt and his senior friends prove that there are still new adventures and opportunities for senior citizens. We can't wait for the next set of adventures! Go get 'em Walt! Lee & Marilyn, Santa Maria, CA

****

Another awesome mystery/ comedy from Robert Thornhill!

The mark of a really excellent author (in my opinion) is one who can bring the characters to life in such a way that I laugh with them and cry with/for them. Robert Thornhill does this.

I love Walt and all his friends. They are the type of friends everyone wants in their life. I loved their Thanksgiving dinner celebration. Elizabeth, Lexington, KY.

****

Each book in the Lady Justice series is better than the last, which is saying a lot because the first one was fantastic. Mr. Thornhill has a wonderful sense of humor that he sprinkles liberally throughout his stories. If you have a grandfather, a dad in his retirement years, or you yourself are of the AARP generation you will not be able to hold back your laughter as you read your way through the Lady Justice series. Can't wait for the next installment! Barbara, La Porte, IN.

****

This book was such a cute light read. I didn't have to try to remember who all the characters were or how difficult the plot was. I just got to read it and enjoy it. I could put it down and come back and easily remember where I was.

Some novels I have to backtrack to remember characters and plot. With this one I just laughed 'til I cried and loved the crazy people. I look forward to the next installment to see what trouble they would get into the next time. Vicky, Independence, MO.

LADY JUSTICE

AND THE

CLASS REUNION

A Walt Williams
Mystery/Comedy Novel

ROBERT THORNHILL

Lady Justice and the Class Reunion

Published in the United States of America

Cover design by Peg Thornhill

1. Fiction, Humorous
2. Fiction, Mystery & Detective, General

LADY JUSTICE AND THE CLASS REUNION

PROLOGUE

Frank Pollard and Patrick O'Brian waited anxiously for their old friend, Earnest Harding to emerge from the exam room.

"What do you think, Paddy? He's been in there a really long time."

"I want to think the best, Frank, but I fear the worst. He hasn't been his old self for the past few weeks."

"I was counting on your connection with the Man Upstairs to bring us good news."

Father O'Brian could imagine what his friend was experiencing. Just a few months earlier, he had been in that same exam room and received the news that his days on earth were numbered. Shortly after, he retired from the priesthood.

"Unfortunately, Frank, my having been a priest for fifty years doesn't give me any more influence with the Almighty than you --- well, maybe a little more, you being an agnostic and all."

"Now, Paddy, you know as well as I that I'm not denying the existence of a Higher Power. I'm just one of those guys that has to see it to believe it. A good report from Ernie would certainly help convince me."

"There you go again, Frank. What you want is proof, but what you need is faith --- the assurance of things hoped for, the conviction of things not seen, Why I ---"

"Hold that thought, Paddy. Here he comes."

The two friends watched as Earnest padded across the reception room floor.

"Well?"

"Well, what, Frank?"

"Cut the crap, Ernie. We've been sitting out here two hours. We're not looking for a weather report. What did Doc Johnson say?"

"I think I'd rather talk about the weather. I'm afraid my forecast is a bit gloomy."

Frank and Paddy exchanged glances.

"So it's not good news."

Ernie shook his head. "Looks like the cancer has spread to my pancreas. The Doc thought we had it whipped, but it's back --- big time! Well, Paddy, I guess you and I will be riding off into the sunset together. He's giving me six months --- tops.

Ernie turned to Frank. "So as of today, you're the only one of the Three Amigos that hasn't got their ticket to the Promised Land punched. I hope you're not feeling left out."

"I'm so sorry, Ernie. It's just not right to lose both of my best friends at the same time. Paddy, maybe you can see why I'm a little short on faith right now."

"Of course I understand, Frank. You seem to be taking the news harder than Ernie."

"Yeah, how about that, Ernie? You don't seem to be too upset."

"Hey, I've had a good run. Eighty-five years, a beautiful wife and two wonderful kids. What more can a man ask for? Nobody lives forever. Anyway, Martha's been gone five years now and I miss her. How about it, Paddy? Will I get to see her on the other side?"

"I believe you will, Ernie, I ----."

"Hang on a dang minute," Frank interjected. "You guys are talking like you've already been planted. Six months! We've got six more months together and I figure we need to make the most of it. You're not going to throw in the towel on me, are you?"

“We’re just being realistic,” Ernie replied. “We’re all in our eighties, the monthly fees at Whispering Hills have pretty much tapped out our savings and all three of us are in bed at nine o’clock every night. Exactly what did you have in mind?”

“I --- I don’t know. I just know I’m not ready to give up and say that it’s all over. Don’t either of you have something left undone --- something you always wanted to do before you kick the bucket?”

Paddy and Ernie looked at each other and shrugged their shoulders. “Can’t think of anything offhand,” Ernie said.

“You guys are pathetic!” Frank growled.

Frank shook his head in disgust. "Well, here we are. Dinner's over. Time for the six o'clock news. Then we'll watch a couple of stupid TV shows and hit the sack. Tomorrow, it will be the same thing all over again. I just don't want it to end this way!"

"Like I asked earlier today," Ernie replied, "what do you have in mind?"

Frank looked around the room. How about something carnal? Earl told me that Minnie was a willing lass. Paddy, you're not a priest anymore. Don't you want to dip your wick before you go?"

Paddy grinned. "First of all, you really don't know whether my wick has been dipped or not, and in either case, when I joined the priesthood, I took a vow of abstinence. I'm not about to renege on that this close to the finish line."

"I should have known. How about you, Ernie? One last fling?"

"Oh sure! When I meet Martha on the other side, I'll be sure to tell her that my dying wish was to bed Minnie Potter. Why don't you take a crack at it, Frank?"

"Honestly, the old tool has been in the shed so long, I'm not sure it still works. Kinda rusty. We're pathetic! We can't go gamble at the casinos because we got no money. I can't drink no more. Every time I have a beer, it gives me gas ---."

"Shhh, quiet!" Paddy said, pointing to the TV set. "I want to hear this."

A reporter was standing outside a Westport

nightclub. “Tonight, the body of a young woman was discovered in the alley behind Kelly’s Westport Inn. The police are not releasing the name of the victim but patrons inside the club are saying the death might have been caused by a drug overdose. If that is the case, this would be the third drug related death in Westport this month.”

Paddy made the sign of the cross.

Ernie saw the look of concern on his friend’s face. “What is it, Paddy? Did you know the woman?”

“No I didn’t know her --- but I know where the stuff came from that killed her.”

“How could you possibly know that?” Frank asked with astonishment.

“Never mind. Forget it. I’ve already said too much.”

“What do you mean, forget it? A woman is dead and you say you know who killed her and we’re supposed to pretend that it never happened? No way! Now spill the beans!”

“I --- I can’t. You wouldn’t understand.”

“I think I do,” Ernie said, putting his hand on Paddy’s arm. “It’s the confessional, isn’t it?”

Paddy nodded his head.

Frank couldn’t believe what he was hearing. “You mean to tell me that some low-life confessed about these drugs and you never reported it to the cops!”

“I knew you wouldn’t understand.”

“Paddy!”

“Calm down, Frank,” Ernie interjected. “Any

information learned in a confessional is privileged and protected by law --- much the same as in a doctor-patient or lawyer-client relationship. If I'm not mistaken, a priest is strictly forbidden to reveal anything he hears in a confessional."

"But ---!"

"Ernie's right, Frank. According to Roman Catholic Canon Law, priests may not reveal what they have learned during confession to anyone, even under the threat of their own death or that of others. For a priest to break confidentiality would lead to automatic excommunication. It's a pretty big deal."

"But people are dying ----!"

"Some already are, including the poor soul that made the confession."

"Wait just a cotton-picking minute," Frank said. "What you're saying is that someone told you about the drugs in the confessional and now that someone is dead?"

"I believe so. Shortly after the confession, this person went missing and hasn't been seen since."

"Probably at the bottom of the Missouri River wearing cement shoes."

Ernie had been quietly listening to the exchange. "Paddy, let me ask you a hypothetical question. I understand about confessional confidentiality, but does it extend to others outside the confessional?"

"You mean like to other people related to the crime?"

"Yes, like that."

A long silence.

"I think I see where you're going and it could be a really gray area. Let me think about that for a minute."

"Well I get it," Frank said. "What's there to think about? This poor schlup gets hooked up with a drug dealer, has second thoughts and spills his guts to a priest. The drug dealer sees the guy getting shaky and offs him. I can see you protecting the guy that confessed, but what about the dealer? Now he's probably a murderer too. What's to stop you from taking everything you know to the cops?"

"And when I sit down with a detective, he is going to want to know where I got the information. If I tell him the truth, then I've violated the confessional sanctity. If I don't, I have nothing to back up my story."

"Yeah, I can see where that could be a problem."

"So," Ernie said, "in the confession, you learned about not only the perpetrator, but his operation as well?"

"Yes, there was quite a bit of detail."

"Then what we need to do is to somehow draw the attention of the police to this dealer and leave enough evidence to make them investigate without revealing anything about your confessor. Would that be acceptable within the framework of your Canon Law?"

"You know, I believe that it would."

"Then I think we have our work cut out for

us, and we've got six months to get the job done. What do you think, Frank?"

A big grin spread across Frank's face. "Now that's what I'm talking about!"

CHAPTER 1

My name is Walter Williams.

I'm a sixty-nine-year-old cop that just returned from a seven day Alaskan Cruise with my wife, Ox my partner, and his new bride, Judy.

It was their honeymoon and Maggie and I had been invited to join them for the week, relaxing aboard a luxury liner, enjoying good food and sitting in deck chairs marveling at the beauty of the Alaskan wilderness.

Naturally, it turned out to be anything but that.

Somehow, fate had seen to it that 'relaxing' was never on our itinerary.

A double murder our first night on the high seas led us into a century-old mystery.

During the week that we were supposed to be relaxing, we were almost blown to bits --- twice, we were thrown off of a moving train and nearly skewered in our sleep by deranged gold thieves.

After miraculously surviving all of that, we boarded our plane in Anchorage and arrived back in Kansas City twenty-two hours later.

Thinking that we would return rested and revived, we had scheduled our return to work the next day --- in retrospect, a bad decision.

After a mere three hours of shut-eye, I stumbled out of bed and into the shower. Somehow I managed to shave without slitting my throat. I threw on my uniform, climbed into my car and headed for the closest Starbucks.

Maggie was still sawing logs when I left --- one of the perks of being a self-employed real estate agent.

Ox and I dragged ourselves into the squad room just minutes before Captain Short entered the room.

Of course, the squad wiseacre, Officer Dooley, noted our entrance immediately. "Welcome back, guys. By the way you both look like crap. I know honeymoons can be exhausting, but, I figured guys your age ---."

Thankfully, the Captain entered, cutting off any further comments from Mr. Dooley.

"Good morning, men, and welcome back Walt and Ox. I'd like the two of you to see me after the meeting."

Ox and I both slumped in our seats. Every other time the Captain had requested a private audience, we had been 'volunteered' for some special assignment --- usually undercover, and usually something no other officer would touch. What he had in store for us this time was anybody's guess.

After the squad meeting, we were ushered into the Captain's office.

"The timing of your return is perfect. After a restful week away from the squad, I'm sure you're ready for your next assignment."

I thought I heard Ox moan.

"Well --- uhhh ---- actually, we're still a little jet-lagged," I stammered. "Any chance we could start this thing tomorrow?"

"What! And waste a day? I don't think so. We need to nip this thing in the bud. Someone's been ripping off the members of the Beautiful Bodies Health and Fitness Club. They're breaking into lockers in the men's dressing room, stealing cash and jewelry, and somehow getting away without a trace."

"So you want us to do ---- what, exactly?" Ox ventured.

The Captain handed each of us a plastic card. "You'll both be working out at the Health Club --- every day until we catch this guy. We're assuming that it's a guy since all of the thefts have come from the men's locker room. Use the machines, the weights, the treadmill, the pool --- whatever you want. Just keep your eyes open and check on the locker room when you see people coming and going."

"Why us?" Ox asked. "Neither of us are exactly a fitness center type of guy. Seems like a couple of the younger fellows --- you know --- the muscle-bound guys that work out regularly would be a better fit."

"That's exactly the point," the Captain replied. "Those apes would be intimidating. You guys --- not so much. Besides, you're both all rested from your vacation. Look at it this way. Ox, you could stand to lose a few pounds and Walt, a man your age needs to stay limber to ward off the arthritis. Think of it as an extended vacation. You get all the perks of Club membership and we catch a bad guy in the process. Now off you go."

Out in the hall, Ox slumped into a chair. "When the alarm went off this morning and I drug my butt out of bed, I figured I was half dead. If I gotta go work out, it's gonna finish the job."

"Look on the bright side," I replied. "Maybe they have a hot tub. We could take turns."

"Walt, you're always the optimist. That's why I like you."

"Looks like we'll both need to go home and pack our gym bags. Shorts, athletic shoes, swimsuit, jock strap --- not exactly my idea of a fun time, but at least I don't have to dress up as a transvestite on this assignment."

That brought a smile to Ox's face. "Yeah, that's a picture I'll never get out of my mind. Good times!"

"See you at the pool."

By the time I returned home, Maggie was up and padding around the apartment in her robe and fuzzy slippers.

I had stopped by Starbucks again, and having swallowed my second Macho Grande with two squirts of espresso, I was beginning to almost feel human again.

Maggie was still in a jet-lagged stupor.

She reminded me of one of my grandmother's old sayings, "You look like you were drug through a knothole backwards."

"What are you doing home this time of day?" she mumbled. "I just got up to pee and I'm heading back to bed."

I knew I shouldn't have done it, but sometimes I just can't help myself.

"That's perfect! I'm on my way to an assignment and I have a little time to spare. How about a quickie?"

Actually, in her present condition, that was the farthest thing from my mind.

Her first reaction was bewilderment --- like I had asked her to sprout wings and fly. In an instant, as my request sunk in, the bewilderment turned into resentment. "I can barely walk and you expect me to ---- "

Then she saw me smile and the resentment turned into sarcasm. "You jerk! If you're looking for sex, why don't you just go ---!"

"Just kidding! Just kidding!"

She shook her head in disbelief and collapsed on the couch. "So what are you doing home?"

I told her about our fitness club stakeout.

That brought a smile to her face. "My Walt? Lifting weights? Running laps? This will probably be your most dangerous assignment yet. You'll probably drop something on your foot. Actually, with your little joke, you'll fit right in with the other dumbbells."

I could see that I wasn't going to get a lot of sympathy from my sweetie. That ship had sailed.

I packed my stuff in my gym bag, tucked Maggie in bed and headed out the door.

I live on the top floor of my three-story apartment building. There are four other one-bedroom apartments occupied by my Dad, Bernice, his current squeeze, the Professor and Jerry. My old friend and maintenance man, Willie, lives in an efficiency apartment in the basement.

I had hoped to escape without encountering any of my tenants, especially Jerry. He's really a sweet guy, but he fancies himself as a stand-up comic --- so much, in fact, that we have dubbed him, 'Jerry The Joker'.

He is a regular on amateur night at the local comedy club and is constantly testing new material on his poor neighbors.

As luck would have it, Jerry was sitting on the front porch. He spotted my gym bag right away.

"Looks like you're either working out or running away from home."

I really didn't want to get into the whole undercover thing, so I confirmed that I was heading to the fitness center.

I could see him mentally sorting through all of the funny stuff he had stored in his brain.

"Did you hear about the chubby lady that had

to give up jogging? Her thighs kept rubbing together and set her pantyhose on fire!"

"Well, I don't wear pantyhose, so that's one thing I won't have to worry about today."

Actually, I did wear pantyhose once when I was undercover as the transvestite, but I wasn't about to share that tidbit of information with Jerry.

"I need to hurry. I'm supposed to meet Ox."

"Just one more ---- please!"

"Okay, but make it fast!"

"A blonde is terribly overweight, so her doctor puts her on a diet. 'I want you to eat regularly for two days, then skip a day, and repeat this procedure for two weeks. The next time I see you, you'll have lost at least five pounds.

When the blonde returns, she's lost nearly 20 pounds. 'Why, that's amazing!' the doctor says. 'Did you follow my instructions?'

The blonde nods. 'Absolutely! But I'll tell you, I thought I was going to drop dead that third day.'

'From hunger, you mean?' asked the doctor

'No, from skipping.'"

I could tell that he was about to launch into another one when Willie walked onto the porch.

"Oh, hi Willie. Jerry was just about to share a joke. Tell him, Jerry."

I hated to do that to my old friend, but a man has to do what a man has to do.

As Jerry forged ahead, I heard Willie mutter, "I get you for dis, Mr. Walt!"

Ox and I pulled into the parking lot at the same time.

We grabbed our gym bags and headed to the reception desk.

A cute young thing greeted us. "May I have your cards, please?"

We fished around in our pockets for the plastic membership cards that the Captain had given us.

She swiped the cards and handed them back. "Have a good workout," she said cheerily.

"Good workout, my ass!" he muttered.

I could see that Ox hadn't quite recovered from our ordeal. I figured his two hundred and thirty pound body took more time to adjust than my one hundred and fifty pounds.

We followed the arrows around the indoor track to the men's locker room.

"You know," Ox said, "I was wondering on the way over here why they just didn't put up surveillance cameras. If that didn't stop the guy, they would at least have him on film."

We arrived at the door and I pointed to a sign displayed prominently with big letters.

"NO CAMERAS OF PHOTOGRAPHY EQUIPMENT OF ANY KIND ALLOWED IN THE LOCKER ROOMS. ANY VIOLATIONS SHOULD BE REPORTED TO MANAGEMENT

IMMEDIATELY."

"That's why. I guess the members have an expectation of privacy and the thief takes advantage of it."

As soon as we entered the locker room, I discovered another reason why there should NEVER be cameras there.

A half dozen guys were parading around in various stages of undress. Everywhere you looked there were buns flapping and weenies wiggling. It wasn't a pretty sight.

"Not the best place to be if you have modesty issues," I said.

Ox pushed me along. "Let's get dressed and get out of here. I saw that hot tub you mentioned. Mind if I take the first dip?"

"Be my guest."

Ox donned his swimsuit, I put on my T-shirt and gym shorts and we were off to our new assignment.

As I looked around the workout area, there seemed to be three distinct classes of people.

The smallest group consisted of the hot bodies that had obviously been sculpting their physiques for many years. They were entirely focused on their tasks and I noted that some of the guys were lifting weights bigger than me.

The second group was the folks whose bodies had probably been sculpted by Ronald McDonald. They ranged from the overly plump to the morbidly obese. Their use of the various machines seemed to be geared more toward sitting than working out. Most of them had a blank stare on their face and you could almost hear them whispering, "Why am I doing this?"

The third and largest group was the seniors. They ranged in age from the fifties to the eighties. I figured I fell somewhere in the middle. Most of them were either on the treadmills or one of the rowing machines, trying to get the old joints loose and limber.

I watched one woman who had to be in her late eighties peddling one of the rowing machines in sloooow motion. It brought to mind something I had read, "It is well documented that for every mile that you jog, you add one minute to your life. This enables you, at age 85, to spend an additional 5 months in a nursing home at $5,000 per month."

Something to look forward to.

I noticed that most of the folks were carrying around paper towels that they had saturated with some pink stuff that was in spray bottles at several locations. They dutifully wiped the equipment before using it and again after they had finished.

I was wondering about the significance of this little ritual when I spotted a young kid about to work out with the curl bar.

He reached for the bar, hesitated, covered his nose and mouth with his hands and sneezed, then picked up the bar and started curling.

It immediately brought to mind a little ritual that Maggie and I have when we go grocery shopping. We always wipe the cart handle with one of those disinfectant wipes. I have a little ditty that I recite that helps me remember to do it. I figured that I should probably adapt my ditty to the gym.

I boogied in the parking lot
I boogied in my car
I boogied on my finger
And I wiped it on the bar.

It occurred to me that if I was a terrorist and I wanted to spread a deadly contagion, a health club might be a dandy place to start.

I made a mental note to share my ditty with Ox.

I hefted a few of the smaller dumbbells and smiled as I remembered Maggie's comparison.

I watched as men entered and left the locker room. It seemed that most of the time there were at least three or four guys in there. That obviously wouldn't be the best time for the thief to do his dirty work.

Almost everyone had placed a lock of some description on their locker. The general conception is that a padlock keeps your stuff safe. That's the farthest thing from the truth. In my landlord days, I learned that a good bolt cutter would snap through a lock shackle in seconds. That was what the thief was doing, but he obviously couldn't do it with other guys standing around. He had to pick the moment when the place was empty.

I had also noticed that many of the gym bags were as big as a small suitcase and could easily conceal a bolt cutter.

I wondered about the Club instituting a rule that all bags had to be searched when entering and leaving, but I could see that the logistics would be horrible and we would probably run afoul of unlawful search issues.

Plus, who would want the job of shuffling through a gym bag full of sweaty jock straps?

Any time I thought that the locker room might be nearly empty, I took a look, but so far, everything was on the up and up.

A big, barrel-chested guy sat down on a bench and picked up two huge weights. Something on the other side of the room caught my attention and I looked away.

A few seconds later, I heard, “Arrrrrgh ---- Arrrrrrgh ----- Arrrrgh!”

It sounded like some huge beast was coughing up a hairball. It was the barrel-chested guy. At that moment one of the Club employees walked by.

I grabbed his arm. “Is that guy all right?”

He smiled. “Yeah, that’s just Ron. He’s our drama queen. I guess he thinks all that groaning impresses people. You’ll get used to it.”

About that time, Ox walked up. He was all pink and wrinkly from stewing himself in the hot tub.

“If you were a lobster, I’d say that you’re ready for the table.”

“Very funny. Anything going on?”

"Arrrrrgh ---- Arrrrrgh ----- Arrrrgh!"

Ox nearly jumped out of his skin. "What the hell?"

"Just another day at the gym."

"So, do you want your turn in the hot tub?"

I looked at his shriveled fingers. "No thanks. I'll pass."

"I'll get changed and see you back here in a few minutes."

I had seen a guy go into the locker room with a kid that looked to be about three years old. They came out and the little tyke was carrying a Spiderman gym bag almost as big as he was.

I saw him wave to a woman on the other side of the Club and heard his dad say, "Run over to Mommy while I work out."

We both watched as the kid skipped across the floor. The two disappeared into the women's locker room.

"Cute kid," I remarked.

"Yeah, he is, but he's a handful."

Not ever having kids of my own, I wondered how much longer the boy would be wandering around the women's locker room before he started noticing that there was a difference.

About that time, Ox returned.

He was about to reluctantly pick up a dumbbell when Ron, the drama queen, tapped him on the arm.

"Say, I wonder if you could help me out. All of the benches with the footholds are taken and I need to do some setups. Would you mind holding my feet down?"

Ox saw the request as the perfect excuse to not have to pick up the dumbbell.

"Sure. Why not?"

The big fellow laid on his back on the bench, spread his legs slightly apart and gave Ox the 'thumbs up'.

Ox crouched between Ron's legs and placed his hands over his ankles.

I could see the big man struggle as he tightened his stomach muscles and attempted to raise his massive torso.

I heard the rumble from several feet away. It was just the precursor to the eruption that followed soon after.

Ox had seen it coming too. His eyes grew wide as he realized that he was in the direct line of fire.

The resulting emission was of such magnitude that heads turned halfway across the gym.

Ox slumped to the floor and I heard him mutter, "Good Lord!"

"Sorry about that, man. Must have been the burrito I had for lunch."

Ox struggled to his feet, eyes watering, and staggered in my direction.

"Hey! What about my ankles?"

I peered around Ox. "I think my friend is more concerned with your ass than your ankles right now."

"Fine!"

"When Ox could finally take a deep breath, he wheezed, "What time is it? I gotta get out of here!"

I had just looked at the clock on the wall, when an old gentleman came tearing out of the locker room.

"My wallet's gone! I've been robbed!"

I had been watching and waiting all afternoon and the perp had struck right under our noses.

CHAPTER 2

"Okay, Paddy," Frank said as the three friends huddled in Ernie's apartment at Whispering Hills, "now that we're away from prying ears, what's the scoop on this drug thing?"

Patrick O'Brian looked sternly at his two companions. "I'll tell you what I can without breaking the confessional seal, but you must promise two things."

"Sure! Sure!" Frank replied impatiently. "Anything. Just get on with it."

"First, what I tell you today must remain absolutely confidential. You can't breathe a word to anyone. If someone discovered that I was sharing confessional information --- well--- it could stir up all kinds of problems."

"That's not a problem," Ernie replied. "What else?"

"Don't press me for more than I can give." He looked directly at Frank. "You can be a bit pushy at times, my friend. If I tell you something is off limits, back off!"

Frank raised his hands in a mock defensive posture. "I read you loud and clear, Padre. You're the boss."

"Good! Then here's what I know. A young woman came to me and asked for a confessional and ---."

"So your stoolie was a dame?" Frank said, surprised.

Paddy gave his friend a disgusted look. "Now there's a third condition --- no interruptions!"

"Okay! Sorry!"

"As I was saying, this young woman in my parish asked for a confessional. She was Hispanic and told me that she had been recruited by a man here in Kansas City named Hector Corazon to smuggle cocaine from Mexico to Kansas City."

"A drug mule!" Frank interrupted.

Paddy nodded.

"Oh, sorry! Please continue."

"She was to be given transportation to Matamoros, Mexico where she was to meet with Corazon's supplier. Now comes the sad and disgusting part of the story."

Paddy paused and tried to compose himself.

"The poor girl was to have an operation in Matamoros and fitted with breast implants filled with cocaine. They offered her a thousand dollars when she returned to Kansas City and the drugs were surgically removed.

Frank shuddered. "Holy Crap!"

"The promise of that much money was too much to resist, so she agreed, but as the time grew near for her departure, she began to have second thoughts. She came to me the day before she was to leave. She told me that she was not going through with her commitment and that she was going to flee the city. I urged her to go to the police but she feared for her family's safety. No one has seen her since that day."

"I'm not surprised," Ernie said. "The poor girl knew too much. A man like Corazon couldn't leave loose ends lying around."

"I'm afraid I agree."

"So what now?" Frank asked.

Paddy thought for a minute. "It seems to me that we need to gather as much information as possible about this Corazon character and his drug operation. Then we'll know where to start."

Frank and Ernie both nodded in agreement.

"Good. Let's hit the computers in the Whispering Hills Library. Ernie, see what you can find about drugs in the Kansas City area. Frank, check out the Matamoros connection. I'll see what I can dig up on Hector Corazon. Let's nail this guy --- for that poor girl!"

Captain Short was as perplexed as we were. "How could this have happened? Weren't you both at the club?"

"Absolutely, Captain," I replied. "I was in the workout area just outside the men's locker room door and Ox was keeping an eye on the pool area."

I left out the part where Ox was probably zonked out in the hot tub.

"The old gentleman that was robbed had been in the pool for about an hour in some kind of aerobics class. During that time there were maybe a dozen men in and out of the locker room. I saw nothing that would arouse any suspicion."

"Then we're missing something," the Captain replied.

"The club is huge and there's so much going on," Ox ventured, "maybe we need a few more eyes."

The Captain shook his head. "I can't spare any more men. This is definitely an annoyance and troublesome to the victims, but we're not talking a major crime spree here. I've got drive-by shootings and a car-jacking I'm dealing with right now."

This wasn't the first time Ox and I had been given 'annoying' assignments where we were basically on our own to come up with a solution. Two of the instances that came to mind were the Gillham Park purse-snatcher and the Senior Center mugger. On both of those occasions, we had enlisted the aid of my friends at my apartment.

"Uhhh, Captain, I think I might know where we can get a few more eyes into the club."

The Captain rolled his eyes. "I suppose you're talking about the 'over-the-hill-gang'?"

"You have to admit they have a pretty good track record. All they'll have to do is keep their eyes peeled for anything that looks suspicious. Ox and I will be right there if things get dicey."

The Captain thought for a moment. "Then I guess you'll be needing more membership cards."

I called Maggie and asked her to assemble the troops in our apartment. She wasn't thrilled with idea. I couldn't imagine why.

It was an interesting group that had gathered in my apartment and was anxiously awaiting my arrival.

Three were octogenarians; my Dad, a retired, over-the-road trucker, who had been banished from his retirement village for lascivious behavior; Bernice, a little wisp of a woman who had become Dad's paramour soon after he arrived, and the Professor, my mentor from my college days at the University.

Willie, my old friend, who had left a life of crime on the streets to become my maintenance man, and Jerry, our self-proclaimed comedian, were in their late sixties.

Anyone that says that life in the twilight years is dull and meaningless has never met this crew.

Maggie met me at the door. "Well, Columbo, you've certainly stirred up a hornet's nest. I hope you know what you're getting into."

Dad was the first to speak. "I'm ready for a new case. It's been dull around here since we whacked that Bondell creep. What's our assignment?"

I launched into my explanation, and I should have known from the opening exchange that I had my hands full.

"We'll all be going to the gym."

Bernice, who had obviously forgotten her hearing aid, raised her hand. "Who's Jim?"

"No, Bernice, gym --- not Jim --- a gymnasium!"

"Ohhhhh,"

After carefully explaining the case and emphatically emphasizing that their involvement was to be totally as observers, they were hot to trot.

Jerry wanted to know if they were going to be deputized and get badges. Willie called him a dipshit.

The Professor was his usual philosophical self and quoted President Kennedy, "Ask not what your country can do for you, but what you can do for your country."

"Heaven help us!" I thought as the troops scattered to gather their gym clothes.

Dad volunteered to drive the crew to the fitness center.

I was on the way when my cell phone rang.

"So what am I, chopped liver?"

"Mary?"

"Hell yes, it's Mary! Ain't I good enough to

be in your little posse?"

"Oh, crap! I forgot about Mary!"

Mary Murphy is the seventy-something housemother at my Three Trails Hotel. She is an imposing two hundred pounds and keeps my ner-do-well tenants in line with a white ash baseball bat.

For a good-hearted, law abiding woman, Mary has compiled quite a rap sheet at the precinct.

She clobbered a hired killer that was about to pull the trigger on Maggie and me, shot an intruder that had threatened her with a knife and whacked a Russian mobster that had me in his rifle sites.

I thought my best defense was to lie. "Actually, I was on my way to the Hotel right now. I have a special assignment for you that I didn't want the others to know about."

Mary let that sink in for a minute. "Well then, I guess that's okay. Special assignment, huh?"

"Uhhhh, yes! Hush, hush stuff. By the way, how did you know ---?"

"I called Willie. Old man Feeney stopped up the crapper again and I needed him to come over with the plunger. He told me to plunge it myself cause he was undercover. That's when I told him that I'd plunge his black ass the next time I saw him."

"No need for violence. The toilet can wait. They have three more. Pack your workout clothes. I'll be there in a few minutes."

I made a u-turn and headed to the hotel, desperately trying to conjure up a special assignment. I certainly didn't want *my* ass plunged.

“So what’s my special assignment?” Mary asked eagerly as she piled into the front seat.

“I need you in the senior’s aerobics class.”

It was the best I could come up with on short notice.

“Aerobics? You mean I gotta bend over and do squats and shit like that? My body don’t do that no more.”

“That’s too bad,” I said with as much disappointment as I could muster. “That’s a critical position and you’re the best I’ve got. I was really counting on you.”

I saw her wince a little. “Well, I guess I could do it --- but no set ups --- they make me fart.”

It seemed that Mary and Ron, the drama queen, had a lot in common.

By the time we arrived and checked in at the front desk, Ox and the rest of the crew were dressed out and ready to go.

I was appalled to see that Dad was decked out in skin-tight, black Speedos that left little to the imagination.

Bernice’s ninety-eight pound frame was barely covered by a two-piece bikini that Dad proudly announced that he had picked up for her at Victoria’s Secret.

“I guess you two are headed for the pool?” I ventured.

“When I heard your dad was going,” Bernice offered, “I figured I’d better tag along. I wasn’t sure I could trust the old goat in a pool full of women in bathing suits."

Given Dad's reputation as a golden aged lothario, she was probably right.

Mary tapped me on the arm and pointed to a group of seniors being instructed by a lithe young woman.

"Is that where I'm supposed to be? If it is, then we got a problem. They're touching their toes. I ain't seen my toes in years. I have to pay Irma Krug five bucks to trim my toenails. Anyway, if God had wanted us to touch our toes, he woulda put 'em on our knees."

Bernice raised her hand proudly. "I can touch my toes."

Dad couldn't resist. "Touching them with your boobs doesn't count."

Bernice punched him in the arm.

Ox shook his head and whispered, "So this is our secret weapon to bring this thief to justice?"

I was beginning to have second thoughts myself.

Our little group dispersed to their posts.

The Professor found a low-impact rowing machine and nodded to the gray-haired lady on the machine next to him. "Good morning, my dear. May I join you?"

Jerry wandered over to a rack of dumbbells. The sign on the rack read, "Free weights."

He stood there for a moment with a puzzled look on his face, then turned to a guy that had just walked up. "Does this mean I can take one home?"

I was just glad that the Captain wasn't there.

Patrick O'Brian poured cups of dark, black coffee as his two friends joined him at his kitchen table.

"Okay, what have we learned? Ernie, you go first. What's the drug story in Kansas City?"

"It's an ongoing battle, I'm afraid. My niece's husband is a cop. I bought him a six-pack one evening and picked his brain. It seems that a lot of the street drugs come from Mexico. Years ago, it was easy to smuggle the stuff across the border into the states, but the Mexican president agreed to a joint operation with the U.S.. It was successful enough that the drug lords had to come up with another scheme.

"It was pretty ingenious. The drugs would be shipped from Mexico across the Gulf to New Orleans. There, they would be buried under tons of sand on barges that were towed up the Mississippi, then onto the Missouri River. The barges would meet their contacts at isolated spots along the river or dock at ports along the way. The sand containing the drugs would be scooped off of the barges into dump trucks and taken to the dealer's distribution center."

"Wasn't there a big shoot-out down by the riverfront a few months ago?" Frank asked.

"Sure was," Ernie replied. "A fisherman spotted a drug exchange and reported it to the authorities. They set up surveillance along the river and nabbed a guy after such an exchange. The guy spilled his guts and that led to the big shoot-out. Thousands of dollars of drugs were seized along with several of the Kansas City drug lords."

"So that pretty much closed the river pipeline into the city, I'm guessing," Paddy said.

"You got that right, but with these guys, if you cut off their supply one place, they'll just find another. That's how this hiding drugs in implants got started."

"That's quite a switch," Frank said. "I can see them shipping tons of the stuff on barges, but how much can you pack into a couple of boobs?"

"Funny you should ask. I have the answer. A Panamanian woman was recently arrested at the Barcelona airport. She had been given implants that contained three pounds of pure cocaine. The stuff is worth about $35,000 a pound. Do the math. That's over a hundred grand."

"Wow! That's some high-priced tittys!"

"And they were going to give your poor girl a thousand dollars to endure all of that pain and humiliation," Ernie said, "if she lived long enough to collect it."

"Okay, Frank," Paddy said, "what's with this Matamoros connection?"

"Matamoros is right on the Gulf coast and is directly across the Rio Grande River from Brownsville, Texas.

"It has been a drug hot spot for years. Being

right on the border, it was the perfect spot to smuggle drugs across the river into Texas, but that deal that Ernie was talking about, with the Mexican president, brought an end to that. There is an ongoing battle between the cartels and the Mexican military in that area and the U.S. Consulate has warned travelers to avoid that part of Mexico.

"Then, being on the coast, it was also the perfect spot to launch the boats that were carrying the drugs across the Gulf to New Orleans. Now that has been nipped in the bud, so apparently, their next scheme is this implant thing. Hard to keep a good cartel down. What about Corazon, Paddy? I'll bet he's from Matamoros!"

"So it would seem. He's new to Kansas City. He bought a huge gated estate in Sunset Hills, just south and west of the Country Club Plaza. I drove by the place and I could see several Hispanic men patrolling the grounds, most likely armed to the teeth. Several of the Kansas City kingpins were taken out of the picture at that riverfront bust. I don't think there's any doubt that this guy was shipped in to fill the void. He's undoubtedly the new drug lord in Kansas City, and we're going to take him out!"

The morning went by without incident.

After her aerobics class, Mary huffed over. I could see that she was in a dither.

"The nerve of that little tart! She was barkin' orders like a drill sergeant. All I said was, 'Back off! This ain't no commando training camp.' She got her panties in a wad and told me I was disruptin' the class, so I told her to bite me."

I guessed that after our assignment was over, they would be revoking Mary's membership card.

"Mary, why don't you ride the stationary bike for a while. That way you can keep a eye on that row of machines."

"A bike? I haven't been on a bike in years. I'd fall right on my butt."

"These bikes don't tip over --- no balance required --- OR --- I think there's an advanced aerobics class about to start."

"Okay, okay. I'll do the bike."

As she mounted the thing and started pedaling, I heard her mutter, "Don't know why I'm doing this. It don't take me nowhere."

About that time Jerry walked up lugging a heavy round object.

"This is the lousiest basketball I've ever seen! It must weigh twenty pounds and it won't dribble."

"That's because it's not a basketball. It's a medicine ball."

"So what's it good for?"

"People toss it back and forth or up in the air. I've seen guys hold it on their chests and do set-ups. Here, let me show you."

As soon as I tossed the heavy ball, I knew it was a mistake. Jerry weighs about a hundred and ten pounds and when he wears his bow tie, he looks a lot like Mr. Peepers.

To his credit, he caught the ball and hung on, but his momentum carried him backwards and he was about to take a header over a weight bench when Ox ran up and grabbed him.

"That's it!" he said, stalking off. "I'm putting in for hazardous duty pay!"

"Hey, partner," Ox said, pointing to his watch. "I think we neglected a very important detail in our undercover operation."

"Oh really? And what might that be?"

"Lunch!"

I should have known that the big guy with the big appetite would be the first one to contract a case of the munchies, but he was right, of course.

"We can't just pack up and head to the nearest burger joint," I said. "It'd be just our luck that the guy would hit the place while we were gone."

Naturally, Ox was ready with a solution. "Pizza! We could order in pizza!"

"That definitely could work," I replied. "I'll get my cell phone and order. You round up the gang."

We had all congregated on some benches in a small reception area in the front of the club.

I could only imagine what was going through the minds of the other club members as they watched two old dripping people wrapped in towels, one in a Speedo and the other in a bikini, a robust woman in leopard spotted leotards, a tall old guy with bony knees and my portly partner, Ox.

"Everybody hungry?" I asked.

"Not me," Willie said. "Havin' to look at yo daddy's junk poking out o'dat thing he's wearin' kinda took my appetite away. Anyway, somebody outta be watchin' in dere. I'll do it, an' if dere's anything left, I'll eat later."

I really couldn't blame him. More than once, when their towels had slipped open, I had to avert my eyes.

Soon, the pizza guy walked in the door carrying three large pies, a box of wings and sodas. I wondered if this was a first for him --- a delivery to a fitness club.

I cringed as I forked over sixty bucks including the tip. I figured I didn't have a snowball's chance of getting reimbursed by the Captain.

Soon, the aroma of hot pepperoni and cheese was wafting through the exercise room. Heads turned and we got dirty looks as the dedicated folks laboring to lose pounds and trim their bodies watched as we wolfed down huge slices, dripping with melted cheese.

When we were finished and the trash had been stowed, Mary announced that she was through with the stationary bike. "Can't do that no more. The inside of my thighs is all chafed and red."

I remembered Jerry's joke and I was glad Mary wasn't wearing pantyhose. They would have probably burst into flame.

"We're heading back to the pool," Dad said.

Bernice giggled as he slapped her on the butt and led her away.

When Dad and his bulging Speedos were out of sight, Willie walked up.

"You all save me any pizza?"

"Sure did," I replied. "Three slices in that box over there. Anything going on in the club?"

"Nope. Pretty quiet. Some guy went in de locker room wit' a little kid. Heard him call the kid, 'Forest'. Wot kind of dad names dere kid Forest?"

Jerry could spot a straight line from a mile away.

"I certainly hope they never take him into the woods. If he got lost they would never find Forest for the trees."

Willie looked at him in disgust. "Man, you is jus' sick!"

Jerry never missed a beat. "Why thank you very little."

I noticed that the Professor was looking a little queasy.

"Are you all right?"

"Just a bit too much grease on top of all that exercise. I have some antacid tablets in my locker. I'll be okay."

I watched as my little gang of health club misfits headed off for an afternoon of surveillance. I had heard veteran officers talk about doing police work 'by the book'. I doubted that our little operation was anywhere near that book.

I found a spot just outside the men's locker

room and was pretending do some curls with a three-pound dumbbell when the Professor emerged.

"Walt, it seems that my locker has been burgled. My wallet is missing."

"Was there anyone in there?"

"Just the man with the little boy."

About that time, the man and the kid came out of the locker room, and just like the day before, I heard the man say, "You go over to Mommy, so I can work out."

The boy was carrying the same Spiderman gym bag.

He waved to his mom and headed across the room to join her.

"No! Who would suspect a three year old boy?" I thought. *"Exactly! Who would suspect a three year old boy?"*

The perfect cover!

The lad had to pass right by me on the way to his mom. I had a dilemma. If I stopped the kid and I was wrong, I could see a lawsuit in my future. If I let him go, the three of them might get away with another heist. I opted for the middle ground.

"Hi son," I said as he approached. "That's really a cool gym bag. I really love Spiderman. Could I take a look at it?"

He stopped and gave me a bewildered look. It occurred to me that he might not have known what 'cool' meant.

"My dad told me never to talk to strange men."

"Your dad was absolutely right, but I'd really like to take a look at your bag."

Instead of handing it over, he rared back and kicked me right on the bony part of my shin.

I winced and made a grab for him, but he took off toward his mother.

I heard his dad yelling, "Run, Forest! Run!"

I limped after him, shouting, "It's them! It's them!"

It wasn't very creative, but it got the attention of my cohorts.

By this time, the kid had reached his mom. She grabbed the bag and ran in one direction and the kid took off in another. It looked like they had rehearsed their getaway plan. I noticed that the dad had headed toward the pool and was probably going for the emergency exit at the far end.

Ox was right behind him and closing fast. The guy stopped, picked up one of those medicine balls and hurled it at Ox. The big guy put up his hands, but just a second too late. The heavy ball hit him right in his gut that was filled with pizza and wings.

I heard the 'Whooof' as the air left his body and my friend collapsed in a heap.

Dad had witnessed the whole affair through the glass that separated the exercise room from the pool. He had correctly surmised that the perp was headed for the emergency exit.

I watched in amazement as the old guy grabbed one of those lifesaving rings attached to a long rope that they throw to people that have fallen overboard.

He swung the thing in circles over his head, and just as the perp past by, gave the thing a fling.

It landed in front of the fleeing man. His feet tangled in the rope and his momentum took him forward right on his face. Dad was on him in an instant and wrapped the rope around the guy's ankles.

Just before my attention was diverted to the mother, I saw Bernice kick the guy in the ribs.

The mom had headed for the front entrance, but stopped short when she saw the menacing face of the big woman in spandex leotards blocking her way.

She reversed her course and was heading toward the pool when a wiry little black man and the reincarnation of Mr. Peepers blocked that route.

She headed to the women's locker room. I knew that if it was like the men's side, there was another door from the showers to the pool area.

Mary was right on her tail. As she followed the woman inside, I heard her yell, "I got this!"

A moment later, I heard the woman's voice screaming, "Get off me, you crazy old bitch!"

Two down and one to go.

I looked around and saw the boy crouching behind one of the machines.

I tried to approach him in a non-threatening way, but I'm sure after seeing his parents brutalized by a gang of old people, he was not in a trusting mood.

He took off and zigzagged in and around the treadmills, bikes and rowing machines.

I would be on one side, with him on the other. I would go one way and he would go the opposite. The little guy was just too quick and slippery. I was getting winded and I could feel the pepperoni creeping up in my throat.

We were at a standoff on either side of a stationary bike. I could see him reading my eyes, ready to take off as soon as I made my move.

An idea popped into my head. I had tried it once with an adult and wound up flat on my back. I didn't think that the kid could whip me, so what did I have to loose?

I pointed to the boy's shoes and with all of the parental caring I could muster, said, "Forest, be careful. Your shoe's untied. You might fall and hurt yourself."

Like most kids that have been warned repeatedly by parents to do this or that, he dutifully checked out his shoelaces.

That one moment was just enough for me to reach around the bike and grab him by the collar.

Apparently, some diversions are age specific.

Once the fitness center thieves were safely on their way downtown in the paddy wagon, our little group gathered in a victory huddle.

"What a day!" Jerry said. "Who would have ever figured that a three year old could be part of a gang?"

I think the Professor summed it up the best.

"Life is like a box of chocolates. You never know what you're going to get!"

CHAPTER 3

"So how do we play this?" Frank asked. "We know who the bad guy is and we know where he lives. What's our next move?"

"I know one thing for sure," Ernie replied. "We need help. Those Mexican drug thugs are mean dudes. I remember reading about that shoot-out on the riverfront. They wore Kevlar vests and carried automatic rifles. They even had a grenade launcher. I think we have to get the police involved."

"So how do we do that without spilling the beans about Paddy's confessional?" Frank asked. "Any thoughts, Padre?"

"I've been kicking an idea around," the old priest replied, rubbing his chin. "Everything would have to work out just perfect, but it would be somewhere to start."

"Then let's hear it. I'm ready to go."

"Let's start with a 911 call saying there has been a home invasion at Corazon's address. The cops will respond to take a look ---."

"Hold it right there, Paddy," Frank said. "That's a gated property and those goons walking the grounds aren't going to let a couple of cops waltz right in."

"You're exactly right, Frank. This is the part where we hope they've sent some officers that have some street smarts. Any cop worth his salt would be suspicious and try to determine who placed the bogus call."

"I'm still not getting it."

"The 911 operator has a record of the location where the call was placed. If we have a couple of sharp cops, they will check out that location and try to find the caller."

"That's a mighty big 'if'!" Frank replied skeptically. "So let's say they do follow up. How does that help us?"

"We'll use a public pay phone. When they show up, we'll have a letter waiting for them, tipping them off to what we know. They'll have the information we have, but won't be able to actually question us."

"I don't know. It's pretty thin."

"Do you have a better idea?" Ernie asked.

"Well ---- no."

"Then let's get started on that letter."

I could see that Ox was moving quite gingerly as we climbed into our cruiser.

"Am I detecting a case of fitness club withdrawal?"

"I had always heard that those places were

supposed to make you healthy, but after two days on those machines, getting gassed by that Neanderthal and hit in the gut with a medicine ball, I'm beginning to have second thoughts."

"Yeah, except for Mary's chafed thighs, you probably got the worst of the ordeal."

"At least the Captain was happy."

"He sure was. He even offered to reimburse me the sixty bucks that I shelled out for the pizza."

We were headed south on Broadway and had just passed Westport Road when the radio came to life.

"Car 54, what's your 20?"

Ox keyed the mike. "We're just north of the Plaza on Broadway."

"We just received a 911 call that a home invasion is in progress at 685 Sunset Drive. Please respond."

"Roger that. We're on our way."

"Sunset Drive!" I said. "That's a pretty swanky neighborhood. Lots of high-priced homes and old money. Real upper crust."

We took Broadway to Ward Parkway, then wound our way through exclusive Sunset Hills until we came to the address.

The number on the stone pillar said 685, but the driveway was blocked by a heavy-duty iron gate. I noticed a security camera mounted on the top of the spiked iron fence.

"Geez," Ox said. "That thing could stop a tank!"

Before we had even closed our car doors, a Hispanic man was standing at the gate.

Ox nodded to the fellow. "I'm Officer George Wilson and this is my partner, Walt Williams. We had a report of ---."

The man cut him off. "Lo siento. No hablo Ingles. Un momento. CARLOS! La policia!"

A few moments later, a slick-haired man appeared that looked like a young Ricardo Montalban.

"Yes, may I help you?"

Ox went through his introduction a second time. "I'm Officer George Wilson and this is my partner, Walt Williams. We had a report of a home invasion in progress."

The man looked puzzled. "There must be some mistake. There has been no home invasion here. No one has made a call to the authorities."

"This is 685 Sunset Drive, isn't it?" Ox said looking at the number on the stone post.

"It is, but I assure you that no one has called." The man pointed to the fence and the camera. "As you can see, we are quite security conscious here."

"As long as we're here, do you mind if we come in and take a quick look around?"

"Actually, I do. Mr. Corazon is involved in a business conference and has given strict instructions that he is not to be disturbed. I'm sure you understand."

Ox could see that he was being given the brush.

"We won't bother anyone inside. We'd just like to take a look at the grounds and the exterior of the house."

You could almost see the fire in Carlos' eyes, but it lasted just a moment.

"Look, officer, I don't mean to be rude, but no one here asked for help. I'm afraid that if you want to come inside this gate you'll need a warrant. Good day!"

With that, he turned and walked away.

"So much for citizen cooperation," I said as we walked back to the cruiser.

Once inside, I noticed that the 'no Ingles' guy hadn't moved a muscle and was watching our every move.

"Something about this whole thing just doesn't smell right," I said.

"You got that right, partner. Did you happen to notice the bulges under those guy's jackets? They were packing for sure."

"Yes, as a matter of fact, I did notice, and I was afraid that if you provoked that Carlos guy one more time, he might show us his. If they didn't make the 911 call, then who did?"

"Let's find out," Ox said, picking up the mike. "This is car 54. Shirley, are you there?"

"Go ahead, Ox."

"We responded to your home invasion on Sunset Drive, but we were told quite emphatically that there was no problem and no one there had placed the call. Can you do a trace for us?"

"Sure thing. Hold on."

We could hear tapping on computer keys.

"Well I'll be damned. They were telling the truth. The call originated from a pay phone. Let me get the location ---- here it is. It came from the Raphael Hotel at 325 Ward Parkway. Of course the guy hung up before I could get a name."

"Thanks, Shirley. We're going to check it out."

"A pay phone," I said, surprised. "Not many of those around anymore."

"Probably in the lobby of the Raphael. That's one swanky place. Let's go see what we can find."

Frank and Paddy were parked a block away from the Sunset Drive estate and watched as the beat up old cruiser pulled into the drive.

Frank gave a disgusted grunt when he saw an old gray-headed cop and his portly partner step out of the car.

"Oh great! For our plan to work we need a couple of sharp cops and they send us Andy Griffith and Barney Fife."

"So who were you expecting? Harry Callahan?" Paddy replied. "Let's give them a chance."

They watched as the two officers spoke through the gate to Corazon's lieutenant.

When the officers turned and headed back to the cruiser, Frank hit the steering wheel with his fist. "I knew they wouldn't get in!"

"Calm down, Frank. We didn't expect them to, now did we?"

"No, I guess not, but I was hoping."

"Look," Paddy said. "The big one's on the radio. Maybe this is going to work after all."

They watched the cruiser pull out of the driveway and head back to Ward Parkway.

"Okay, Frank. Stay with them, but not too close. I'll get Ernie on the line and if they pull into the Raphael, he can plant the letter."

"Ernie? Paddy here. They're headed your way, so get ready. If they turn into the hotel, I'll let you know."

Moments later, the cruiser pulled into the circular driveway of the Raphael.

"Okay, Ernie. They're here! Do your thing!"

Paddy turned to his friend. "See Frank. A little faith can go a long way."

"Wow! This place is gorgeous!" Ox said as we pulled into the drive of the Raphael.

"It used to be the Villa Serena Apartments. It was converted to a hotel in 1975. I read that *Travel and Leisure* voted it as one of the world's best hotels. I had an out-of-town client stay here once. This definitely isn't your Motel 6."

We entered and approached a very proper attendant at the front desk.

"May I help you gentlemen?"

"Yes," I replied. "Could you direct us to your pay phone?"

He pointed across the lobby. "It's down that hall --- on the wall between the two lavatories."

We followed his directions and found an envelope perched on top of the phone. It was addressed to the Kansas City Police Department.

"Well, this is definitely a new one," Ox said picking up the envelope. "What do you think we should do with it?"

"The last time I looked," I replied, "we were the Kansas City Police Department. I think we should open it."

Ox shrugged, gently pried open the flap and pulled out a letter.

I looked over his shoulder and we read together.

To the Kansas City Police Department,

We realize that this is an unconventional way to communicate, but due to issues of confidentiality, we felt that this was the only way to share the information we have without endangering the lives of innocent people.

The owner of the property on Sunset Drive is Hector Corazon.

We have been given information that he is the Kansas City connection to a drug cartel operating out of Matamoros, Mexico.

A reliable source has told us that Corazon is recruiting young women, particularly Hispanic, to travel to Mexico where they have breast implants filled with pure cocaine. Upon their return, the implants are surgically removed.

Although we can offer no proof, there is reason to believe that some of the young women that were recruited may have met with foul play.

If it is not already underway, we hope that this information might lead to an investigation of this blight in our beautiful city.

Sincerely,
Concerned Citizens.

Ox gave a low whistle. "This is way above our pay grade, partner. We'd better take this to the Captain."

On our way out, we stopped at the front desk.

"Pardon me," I said. "By any chance did you see anyone around the pay phone in the last hour?"

"Sorry, officer, but I've been attending to the needs of our guests. I hardly have time to monitor who's coming and going from our lavatories."

"Yeah, I figured as much. Thanks anyway."

As soon as the Captain read the letter, he summoned Sergeant Rocky Winkler of the Drug Enforcement Unit.

Ox and I had worked with Winkler a few months ago at the riverfront shoot-out. He remembered me right away since I was the guy that had almost been blown to smithereens by one of the cartel's grenade launchers.

"Officer Williams. Ever heard the expression, 'Close only counts in horseshoes and hand grenades'?"

It wasn't nearly that funny at the time.

After reading the letter, Winkler just shook his head. "After the river raid, we shut down their main supply line into the city and took their top two men out of commission. We knew it was only a matter of time until they tried something new, but up till now, nothing had come up on our radar."

"Is this implant stuff for real?" Ox asked.

"Oh, absolutely!" Winkler replied. "Just this past week, a Panamanian woman was caught at the Barcelona airport. She had three pounds of pure cocaine in her implants."

"How did they catch her?" I asked.

"It was a botched job. The customs guy saw blood oozing from her blouse and pulled her aside to question her. Her story didn't add up, so they investigated further. This is just the tip of the ice burg. They are using both breast and buttock implants, plus, some of the mules swallow condoms filled with the stuff. One of them died when a packet ruptured in her colon. They found twenty-six bags inside her."

"So unless they see someone bleeding, how do they catch these people?" Ox asked.

"Good question," Winkler replied. "It's difficult, and the way they're doing it makes it even more so. Apparently they're recruiting women that are Hispanic American citizens. There is nothing suspicious about them traveling to Mexico and when they return with the drug implants, since they are American citizens returning home, they are scrutinized less than a Mexican citizen entering the country."

I could certainly understand that. On Ox's honeymoon, we started in Vancouver, Canada. When we departed Canada to get back in the U.S. the process took only minutes.

If our passport was valid, we were in without question.

Winkler continued, "We knew they would be sending a new kingpin to Kansas City, but we didn't know who it would be. If it is this Corazon character, that will give us someplace to start. Any idea who sent this letter?"

"Not a clue," I said.

"Well, we appreciate the information. We'll take it from here. Oh, wait. If you guys want to help, there is one thing you could do."

"What's that?" the Captain asked.

"We have our hands full with the drug end of

things. Maybe your guys could follow up with Missing Persons and see if any young Hispanic girls have been reported missing."

"I think we can handle that. Ox, Walt, see what you can find."

A morning that had started like any other had certainly taken an interesting twist.

CHAPTER 4

Maggie and I were zonked out in our recliners in front of the TV when the phone rang.

Since we were really high tech for a couple of old farts, the caller ID flashed on the screen. "Wanda Bodenhammer".

"I don't know a Wanda Bodenhammer," I said with disgust as the big name blocked my view of Karina Smirnoff's gorgeous legs on *Dancing With The Stars*.

"Me either," Maggie replied.

"Good! Then let's let the machine get it."

"Walt. I might be important. You'd better answer."

"Oh, all right!" I sighed, and picked up the phone.

"Hello."

"Hi --- Walt? This is Wanda."

"Uhhhh ---- yeah."

I already knew that.

"I'm sorry! Wanda Pringle --- it's Bodenhammer now --- from Polk High School."

"Oh, that Wanda. It's been a long time."

Maggie motioned for me to punch the hands-free button.

"Yes, it certainly has --- fifty years! That's what I'm calling about, our fifty year class reunion."

I was immediately on the defensive. "Fifty years! Wow!"

Wanda forged ahead. "The reason I'm calling is that we're forming a committee to plan the reunion and we just knew that you, being a class officer and all, would want to be a part of it."

It was one of those rare moments when I was at a loss for words. If I said I wasn't interested, I would immediately be classified as a jerk, but if I showed any interest at all, I knew I would be sucked into some mind-numbing job.

"Walt?"

"Yeah, I'm here. I don't know, Wanda. I'm awfully busy right now."

"Of course you are. We all are, but surely you could find some time for something as important as your fifty year class reunion."

Maggie punched me in the arm and her lips formed the unmistakable words, "Do it!"

"So when will this committee meet?"

"Thursday evening at six o'clock at the Pancake House. We've reserved a room."

"Swell!" At least I'd get some pancakes out of the deal.

"Oh, great, Walt!" Wanda squealed. "I knew we could count on you."

After Wanda had signed off, Maggie was right on top of the thing.

"I didn't know you were a class officer."

"Well, really just sort of one. I was president of the Beta Club --- the school's honor society."

"You! Honor Society?"

"Hey! I'm not just a pretty face!"

"I'm sorry. I guess I really don't know much about your youth. Do you still have a yearbook?"

"Yeah, I think so --- somewhere in a box in the basement. I haven't seen it in years."

"Then let's go dig it out. You've aroused my curiosity."

"Have I aroused anything else?"

"Go find that yearbook and then we'll negotiate."

Maggie drives a hard bargain.

We scavenged around in dusty old boxes that hadn't been opened since Truman was president and finally found one marked, 'High School'.

Maggie insisted that we drag the whole box up to the apartment and she tore into it like she was unwrapping a Christmas present.

She let out a little squeal when she spied my senior yearbook.

"James K. Polk High. Very impressive! And Wildcats! Wow!"

"It had its downside."

"Care to elaborate?"

"Well, we were the Polk Wildcats. Somebody shortened the name to Polk Cats. Try saying that three times real fast."

She did and then she giggled.

"See," I said, "it comes out Polecats --- the

redneck term for 'Skunk'. Some of my illustrious classmates learned to drink at an early age and earned quite a reputation. Ever here the term, 'drunk as a skunk'?"

She nodded.

"Well that's part of the legacy of my senior class."

She let out another squeal. "Ohh, here's your photo as president of the Beta Club. What's that grave marker on the same page?"

"Another part of my inglorious past. Are you sure you want to hear it?"

"Absolutely!"

"Our Beta Club project that year, under my leadership, was to raise money to plant a memorial tree in the school courtyard. We had a huge ceremony where we dug the hole, planted the tree and I talked about how, in the years to come as the tree grew, it would be the legacy of our class."

"That sounds beautiful."

"Except the next morning, we discovered that someone had chopped the thing down during the night. I always suspected that it was the jocks from the football team, but we could never prove it."

"So what's with the headstone?" **

"We couldn't let the jocks have the last word, so me and a buddy painted that marker and planted it by the stump that night. It said:

**See photo, page 231

R.I.P.
Here lies the Beta tree
Once firm and stout.
It died in great glory
When only a sprout.

"Walt, you are a true leader --- and I LOVE that sexy flat top. What's a girl have to do to get hooked up with the Beta Club president?"

Unfortunately, those were words that I never heard during my high school years, but now, fifty years later, it was music to my ears.

Some things are worth waiting for.

The next morning, Ox and I stopped by Missing Persons and inquired about young Hispanic women that might have gone missing.

The detective on duty looked through his database.

"Not seeing anything. We've had a couple of old geezers wander away from nursing homes, a kid taken by his dad in a custody battle and a sixteen -year-old boy, but he turned up in Las Vegas. All of our other open cases date way back and none of them involve Hispanic women."

We thanked him and as we were heading out to our cruiser, Ox said, "I have another idea. Let's go over to the Sacred Heart Guadalupe Church over on the West side. That church is right in the heart of the Latino community. If anyone would know what's going on, it would be the priest."

We parked in front of the beautiful old church and entered the sanctuary. A young man in priest's robes met us.

"Good morning. I am Father Michael Sebastian. How may I help you?"

"I'm Officer George Wilson and this is my partner, Walt Williams. We've been given some creditable information that some young Latino women are being recruited by the Mexican drug cartel and that at least one has gone missing. We thought that in your position you might have heard something about this."

Father Sebastian looked furtively around the sanctuary and was obviously relieved that no one was in earshot.

"Please, officers. Let's talk in my study."

The Father led us to his study, and I noticed that as he closed the door, he looked both ways to see if anyone had seen us enter.

"I'm sorry, officers, but I may not be of much help to you. I have only been here a few months. My predecessor, Father Patrick O'Brian, had to step down due to ill health. I'm still getting my feet on the ground."

It sounded very much like Father Sebastian was giving us the brush-off.

"I totally understand, Father," Ox said, "but I'm sure you would have heard if one of your parishioners had disappeared under unusual circumstances."

I could see that the priest was struggling with some internal conflict.

"Please understand," he said apologetically, "the church is in a very tenuous position. Yes, I am told certain things in confessional, but anything I hear there is privileged and must remain confidential. The men you are talking about are very dangerous, and the majority of the families in my parish fear them and steer clear of them. Unfortunately, there are some that have not."

"So you have heard of young women that have gone missing?" I asked.

Father Sebastian nodded his head.

"Why haven't these people been reported to the police?" Ox asked. "We checked with Missing Persons and they have no current records of missing Latino women."

"Because the people know that working with the authorities would only bring more reprisals from the cartel. It is better to lose one member of the family than to risk the lives of the entire family. When one becomes involved with these people, there is a price to pay, and sometimes that price is a life."

"So knowing the danger, why would someone get involved with these people in the first place?" I asked.

"You are both white and most likely from middle class families, so you have no idea what it is like for a young Latino boy or girl. Unless they are born into one of the wealthier families, these young women are looking at spending their lives in menial jobs such as a housekeeper at a hotel, barely making enough money to keep food on the table and a roof over their heads. Some try to escape through prostitution; some turn to the cartel. Many of those girls are never heard from again."

"Does the name, Hector Corazon, mean anything to you?" Ox asked.

"Please do not ask me that, Officer Wilson. There are few places in the community that are safe. Places where people may come, worship, and share their burdens. We are a safe haven because we do not make waves in the community. We are here to minister to the needs of the individual. If we become crusaders for reform then we risk jeopardizing the very thing that brings people through our doors. Life is full of choices. We could choose to stand up against the cartels and the misery they bring into the lives of the people or we can choose to bring them God's word and help them make wise choices of their own. I hope you understand."

Without really saying anything, Father Sebastian had pretty much confirmed the information from our anonymous letter writer.

Frank, Ernie and Paddy were parked on the street a half-block from the entrance to the mansion on Sunset Drive.

"Two days!" Frank exclaimed. "It's been two days since we gave our letter to the cops and nothing!"

"So what did you expect?" Ernie replied. "These things take time. All they had to go on was an anonymous letter. They had to check things out on their own. I've read stories in the paper where the cops had surveillance on suspected drug dealers for months before making a move."

"I hope they don't take months this time," Paddy replied. "Two of us may not last that long."

"Well, we might just have to do a bit more detecting on our own," Frank said. "Remember that movie, *The Three Amigos*, with Chevy Chase, Steve Martin and Martin Short. They were fighting a Mexican guy --- hmmm --- if I remember correctly, his name was El Guapo. That's us; the Three Amigos, only we're after Hector Corazon, not El Guapo."

"Yeah," Paddy replied, "but remember, El Guapo didn't have automatic weapons and grenade launchers."

"Yes, there is that!"

At that moment, there was a loud tap on the window. The three men looked up to see a dark-skinned, mustachioed man peering in the window. He gestured for Frank to roll down the window.

"What are you people doing here?"

"We're --- uhhh ---," Frank stuttered, stalling for time to think. "we're with the Sunset Hills

Neighborhood Watch. We're just out on our regular patrol."

The man looked each one in the eye. "I know of no neighborhood watch."

"That's probably because you're new here," Frank continued. "We meet once a month. If you give me your email address, I'll be sure to send you a notice of our next meeting."

The man looked menacingly. "You should move on. You are blocking our street."

Frank was about to protest when Ernie spoke up. "No problem. We have a large area to cover. We'll be on our way."

"See that you do!" the man said and stalked away.

"What? So no email address?" Frank said as he rolled up his window.

"Cripes! Frank!" Ernie exclaimed. "Are you trying to get us shot?"

"Holy Mother of God!" Paddy said. "When he knocked on our window I nearly jumped out of my skin. I think I wet myself. Good thing I'm wearing my Depends."

"Very funny!" Frank said.

"No really," Paddy replied. "Looks like the cancer has spread to my prostate and bladder. Been doing a lot of dribbling, so, yeah, I'm wearing Depends."

"Jesus, Paddy!" Frank said. "I'm sorry. I didn't know."

"Hey, it's no big deal. Shortly after I came

into this old world I started wearing a diaper, so I might as well go out the same way. Listen, we'd better get a move-on before that goon comes back."

Frank started the car and they drove around the block. They were about to make another round when they saw the big iron gates swing open.

"Frank! Pull over!" Ernie said.

They watched as a big black SUV pulled into the street.

"I'll bet that's the man himself," Frank muttered. "What do you think? Should we follow him?"

"Here's something I've been thinking about," Paddy said. "These guys aren't going to have women coming to this swanky address to have bags of cocaine cut out of their breasts. They must have another location where they do their dirty work. I say let's follow them."

"I'm okay with that," Ernie said. "Just don't get too close. One of those goons has seen our faces."

They followed the SUV down Ward Parkway and onto Southwest Trafficway to downtown Kansas City. They wound through the downtown streets until they came to Walnut. They went north on Walnut, which led them into the heart of the City Market district.

A few blocks from the market, they saw the SUV pull up in front of a warehouse. The sign over the door read, 'Aztec Produce'.

"Of course!" Frank exclaimed. "I get it now. When I was doing my research on Matamoros, I learned that agriculture is a big part of the local economy. One of their biggest exports is fruit and vegetables. I'll bet dollars to donuts that this Aztec thing is the legitimate front through which they launder their drug money."

"And I'd make the same bet," Ernie said, "that somewhere inside that warehouse is a surgical bed where they cut the drugs out of those poor girls."

"Looks like it's time for another letter to the cops!"

CHAPTER 5

After squad meeting, Ox and I met briefly in the Captain's office. We reported what we had learned from Missing Persons and from Father Sebastian.

"So basically, what you are saying is that this Corazon character is for real and he is most likely recruiting young women as mules, but you have no evidence to back it up?"

"That's about it, I'm afraid," Ox said. "Are the narcotics guys doing any better?"

"Unfortunately, no," the Captain replied. "I had coffee with Rocky Winkler yesterday. Apparently after the riverfront bust, the cartel has been keeping a low profile. He figures they're staying off the radar so they can get their new pipeline into the city up and running. They found Corazon, but nothing so far to tie him to the Mexican cartel."

"So what now?" Ox asked.

"Right now, that's it for the two of you. You can go back to your regular beat. Just keep your ears and eyes open."

As we headed to our cruiser, I had an idea.

"Do you suppose we could swing by the City Wide Realty office? Maggie has floor duty this morning and she might be able to help us out."

"How so?"

"We know that Corazon just moved into that Sunset Hills mansion fairly recently. It was most likely a listed property. Maggie could do a multiple listing search. It might tell us something."

"It's worth a try."

When we walked in the door, Joan's face broke into a big smile. Joan had been the receptionist/secretary of the company for most of the thirty years I was a salesman there.

"Well, well," she said. "The prodigal son returns. How are you doing, Walt?"

"I haven't been shot at yet today, so I can't complain."

"Bet you're here to see that sweet wife of yours --- that lucky girl."

"You're not flirting with me, are you Joan?"

"Can't help it. I'm a sucker for a guy in uniform. Maggie's in her office."

Maggie was surprised to see us, but recovered quickly.

"I swear I didn't do it, officers. I'm innocent!"

"It's not what you didn't do --- it's what you're about to do." I said, giving her a peck on the cheek. "We need a favor."

"Anything for the men in blue. How can I help?"

"I need you to check on a recent sale --- 685 Sunset Drive."

"Beautiful property!" Maggie said. "I heard it

sold. Let's see what I can find."

She booted up her computer and began tapping keys.

"Yes, here it is. It closed two months ago --- a million and a half --- cash sale."

"Does it say who bought it?" Ox asked.

"No, the buyer's name is not part of the MLS, but I know where we can get it, the Jackson County Tax Database."

She tapped a few more keys.

"Here it is."

"Hector Corazon?" I asked hopefully.

"Nope, a corporation, M.M. Ltd."

"See if they have any other Jackson County holdings."

"Okay, hold on ---- Yes! M.M. Ltd bought a property on 2nd Street in the River Market area about the same time as the Sunset Drive house."

"Yes! Fantastic!" I said, giving Maggie a hug. "That's exactly what we needed. See you tonight."

"Hold on a minute, Buster!" she said, menacingly. "I supply valuable information in an ongoing case and all I get is a 'see you tonight'?"

I had learned that in the male/female relationship, one has to respond quickly and decisively in such situations.

"You are exactly right! (I learned early on to establish that upfront). How does a dinner out at a nice restaurant sound?"

She thought for a moment. "I could live with that."

"Good! Then it's a done deal."

As we headed out the door, Ox said. "You handled that pretty well. You think fast for an old guy."

"Marital Bliss 101. It's a class where you learn from experience."

We were about to leave, when a gal I remembered from one of the title companies walked in the door carrying a big box.

"Hi Joan. I was in the neighborhood so I thought I'd drop off a box of donuts for your break room."

This was one of the perks of pulling floor duty at the real estate office. Some company was always coming in schmoozing us with goodies hoping we would give them our next deal.

Joan took the box and thanked the girl.

"Walt, you and your partner might as well have one for the road.

"Joan, you sure know the way into a man's heart," I said, as we each grabbed a chocolate covered, creme filled long john.

Frank, Ernie and Paddy were sitting in Frank's car outside the precinct garage.

"Paddy, are you sure the car number was 54?"

"Relax, Frank. I may be incontinent but I'm not blind."

"Here comes another one," Ernie said, as a cruiser pulled out onto the street.

"See!" Paddy said proudly. "Car #54 --- and there's the old guy and his portly partner. Don't lose them, Frank!"

Frank started the engine and pulled into traffic a few cars behind the cruiser.

"Bet they stop at a donut shop," Frank said, grinning.

"Don't think I'll take that bet," Ernie said. "I'll bet the big one is on a first name basis with most of the shops in town."

The cruiser passed a Dunkin' Donuts and a Krispy Kreme without even slowing down.

"Shame on you guys," Paddy said. "See what happens when you prejudge people."

They followed until the cruiser turned into parking lot of City Wide Realty. The two cops parked and went inside.

"Okay, this is our chance," Frank said. "I'll pull into that spot away from the front window. Ernie, do your thing and get out of there quick."

Frank parked and Ernie hurried to the cruiser and slipped the envelope under the windshield wiper.

Frank pulled to the far end of the lot and waited for the cops to return.

After about fifteen minutes, they emerged munching on huge long johns.

"Ha!" Frank said gleefully, punching the old padre in the arm. "Tell me about that prejudging thing again."

Paddy just shook his head. "Human nature is a wondrous thing."

They watched as the big one bit into his pastry and a blob of yellow creme squirted out the end and down his uniform shirt.

"Are you sure we picked the right guys?" Ernie asked, skeptically.

"Well, we're stuck with them now. Let's hope for the best."

After pausing to wipe off the goo, the two arrived at the cruiser and spotted the envelope.

The old one looked around then tore it open and began to read.

The three ducked down in their seats.

"That's it," Paddy said. "We've done what we came to do. We'd better skeedaddle before they spot us."

The Three Amigos waited until the two cops went back into the real estate office and quietly drove away.

We were about three steps out the door when Ox bit into his long john and a big glob of vanilla creme squirted out.

This wasn't the first time this had happened. For some reason, Ox has never grasped one of the laws of physics as it relates to pastries: for every action there is an equal and opposite reaction. When you bite down on one end and apply pressure, something usually squirts out the other end.

"Oh, crap!" he said, scooping the errant creme off his shirt with his finger and stuffing it into his mouth.

No point in wasting good creme filling.

I was about to expound on the physics thing when I spotted an envelope tucked under our windshield wiper.

I laid my pastry on the hood and retrieved the envelope. I looked around the parking lot but saw nothing but empty cars.

I tore open the envelope and read aloud to Ox.

To the Kansas City Police Department

Upon further investigation, we have learned that the Mexican drug cartel, led by Hector Corazon, owns a warehouse at 405 E' 2nd Street in the City Market District.

As we mentioned in our previous letter, Corazon has ties to Matamoros, Mexico. One of the chief exports of Matamoros is vegetables. The warehouse owned by the cartel has the sign 'Aztec Produce' over the door.

It is our belief that the produce business in the City Market is a front to launder the cartel's drug money and is possibly the location where the drugs from Mexico are being surgically removed from the poor souls.

We hope this information, along with our previous letter, will assist in your investigation.

Sincerely,

Concerned Citizens.

"Looks like it's from the same people," I said. "Same envelope --- same stationery --- signed the same way. Hang on a minute. I'll be right back."

I returned to the reception desk.

"Joan, did you see anyone around our squad car?"

"Hmm --- the phone has been ringing off the hook, so I've been pretty tied up. Oh, wait. I do remember seeing a glimpse of an old guy walking across the parking lot."

"Define old. Like me old or older?"

"Definitely older than you, but he was so far away that's about all I could tell you."

When I returned, Ox had been studying the letter.

"What are the chances that the very moment we get a lead from Maggie, we also get a letter confirming it. The letter talks about Matamoros, Mexico. What do you bet that M.M. Ltd. stands for Matamoros, Mexico?"

"I'll bet you're right. Let's check it out before we take this to the Captain."

We drove to the City Market District and found the address on 2nd Street. Just as the letter had said, there was a sign above the door, 'Aztec Produce'. The warehouse was huge. It almost covered a full city block.

"There's certainly enough room in there for most anything," Ox said. "Whoever wrote the letter might be onto something."

"Let's have a look around the market before we go back to the precinct. If this is really a front to launder drug money, they have to have a retail outlet."

We parked and started walking the big horseshoe-shaped pavilion that contained the City Market.

There was row after row of vendors selling every vegetable and fruit imaginable. Interspersed between the vegetable vendors were small restaurants offering ethnic food of every description; Italian, Thai, Chinese and, of course, Mexican.

We wandered around until we found the storefront with the 'Aztec Produce' sign. It looked like all of the other vegetable stores except that the workers all appeared to be Hispanic.

Next to the Aztec store was a Mexican restaurant named The Burrito Bandito.

"Colorful name," I said. "Are you thinking what I'm thinking?"

"If you're thinking that maybe we should spend some time sampling their wares while we watch who's coming and going at Aztec, then I'm with you."

"I promised Maggie a dinner out. Do you think Judy would be interested in a double?"

"Hold on, partner. I distinctly remember you

offering Maggie a dinner at a 'nice' restaurant. I'm not sure the Burrito Bandito would qualify."

"Details, details. It's really just the thought that counts."

"We'll see about that!" Ox said.

On the way back to the precinct, I called Captain Short and told him about the second letter. He said Sergeant Winkler would be waiting for us when we returned.

As promised, the Captain and Winkler were waiting in his office.

Sergeant Winkler studied the letter as we shared the details of our morning's adventure.

When we had finished, Winkler said, "Good job, officers. It looks like you have forged a bond with these anonymous citizens. I just have one more question. What do you suppose this dark substance is on the outside of the envelope?"

I had hoped he wouldn't notice.

"Uhhh --- that might be chocolate icing. Sorry."

"So how about that dinner I promised you?" I said as Maggie walked in the door.

"Perfect! After a whole day of floor duty I wasn't real excited about coming home and cooking. Wait! This isn't just an excuse to get me to Mel's Diner is it?"

I tried to look shocked. "How can you even

suggest such a thing?"

Actually, I understood perfectly. At home, our diet consisted primarily of healthy organic stuff, and it was only on those rare occasions that I tricked her into going to Mel's that I got my allowance of grease, gravy and sugar.

"No, Ox and I found a cozy little place today that we thought you girls might enjoy. We're doubling with Ox and Judy if that's okay with you."

"Absolutely! I always enjoy having Judy along. You're not exactly Mr. Conversation. No offense."

"None taken."

Judy, another officer in the KCPD, and Ox had been married less than a year. Maggie and I had been invited to accompany them on their Alaskan honeymoon cruise. During that time Maggie and Judy became close friends.

"So what should I wear? Is this a dressy place?"

It took a moment to find just the right response.

"Walt?"

"Well, actually this place has a more casual atmosphere. I think slacks would be just fine."

Subterfuge is an art.

Ox picked us up in his SUV and we headed downtown.

"So, Judy," Maggie said, "has Ox told you about this special place they're taking us tonight?"

"No, he's been pretty tight-lipped about the

whole thing. Said it was a surprise."

Ox and I exchanged a worried glance."

"Well, it must be pretty special if it's downtown."

The car was silent as we drove past the fancy joints in the new Power & Light District. When we passed The Majestic Steak House in the north part of downtown and Ox kept on driving, Judy said, "Are you sure you know where you're going?"

Ox looked at me pleadingly. "I think we should 'fess up' before we get there. Don't you?"

"Fess up?" Maggie exclaimed. "What have you two cooked up now?"

Reluctantly, I told them the story from the beginning and that our evening out was actually a stakeout to watch a storefront owned by a Mexican drug cartel.

When I finished, the car was deathly silent.

Maggie was the first to speak. "I certainly appreciate your dedication and I'm willing to play along, but if you think for a minute that this fiasco is going to satisfy the dinner out you promised me, you've got another *think* coming!"

Ox leaned over and whispered, "Told you! Marital Bliss 102. You must have skipped that class."

We parked and entered the pavilion.

The combination of aromas emanating from the various ethnic restaurants, combined with the smell of over ripe fruits and vegetables hit us in the face.

"Sheesh! Smells like ass-crack in here!" Ox

muttered.

The Burrito Bandito was about the size of our living room. The outer wall was a huge garage door that could be lowered when the place was closed. There were about a dozen small tables scattered about across from the serving line.

Judy punched Ox in the arm. “Not even a waiter! We have to go through a serving line!”

“Actually, that’s not altogether a bad thing,” Ox said defensively. “You get to choose what you want on your burrito.”

Judy turned to Maggie. “I’d say this place is worth at least two nice dinners out. What do you think, girlfriend?” Maggie gave her a high-five.

Ox leaned over and whispered, “Marital Bliss 103. We should have signed up!”

When it was our turn, a Mexican guy was holding a flour tortilla that must have been eighteen inches in diameter. “Whatcha want?” he inquired.

Ox was first in line and he had the guy load the tortilla with cheese, rice, black beans, Mexican sausage and salsa. When the thing was folded it was the size of a small football.

When we all had our food and drinks, we found a table where we could see the Aztec Produce store.

Every thing looked normal --- just another produce stand. Customers came by, squeezed oranges, sniffed broccoli and paid for their purchases.

I was about halfway through my burrito by the time Ox had wiped the remnants of his off of his mouth. Stuffed, I pushed the rest of mine aside.

"You gonna finish that?" he said, eyeing my burrito.

"Help yourself," I replied.

I watched in amazement as he gobbled the remains of my dinner.

There had been a momentary lull in the restaurant. The employees were just shooting the breeze waiting for the next customer.

I approached and motioned for the Mexican guy that had loaded our burritos.

"You want something else?"

"No, just information. We've been watching the produce store next door. Just wondered if you knew anything about the owners."

The man looked back at his friends with a concerned expression.

"No!" he said emphatically. "We know nothing. They are new. We have nothing to do with them. No more questions."

He turned and joined his friends.

I returned to the table. "That certainly went well."

"They're scared to death," Judy said. "You could see it in their faces."

About that time, a young man brought a skid of fruit from the back of the Aztec store and placed it in front of the bins. A young woman that appeared to be early twenties stepped up to the skid. She tried to lift the first box and we saw her wince in pain. She managed to carry it to the appropriate bin and empty the contents.

When she tried to lift the second box, she winced again and cried out softly.

"That girl is hurting," Maggie said. "Somebody should do something."

"I got this," Judy said.

She walked over to the cash register where an older woman had just rung up a customer.

"Pardon me, ma'am, but it looks like that woman is in pain. You should take a look."

The cashier gestured to the woman, "Maria! Vaya!"

The girl dropped her head and disappeared into the back of the store.

"This is none of your concern," the cashier said. "She will be fine."

Judy isn't intimidated easily. "She sure doesn't look fine."

About that time, a burly Mexican emerged from the back of the store. "We got a problem here?"

"No, no problem," Judy said backing away. "Just trying to help."

We quickly packed up and headed back to the SUV.

"When that poor woman walked by me, she was clutching her breasts," Judy said. "I'd bet anything that she's one of their mules."

"Sure looks like it," I replied. "They send them off to Mexico where they implant them with cocaine, they return and have the stuff cut out and then they make them do manual labor until they heal.

It's horrible!"

"We have to get these guys!" Ox said with conviction.

The ride home was quiet as we each thought about man's inhumanity to his fellow man.

CHAPTER 6

The next evening, when I walked in the door, Maggie was waiting in ambush.

"Okay, Polecat! Hurry and get dressed. We don't want to be late."

I was hoping that she had forgotten the class reunion committee meeting, but no such luck. Maggie seemed intent on delving into my high school history and meeting the classmates of my youth.

"I've been studying your senior yearbook. It appears that you had quite a colorful class."

That was an understatement.

I was in my BVD's when she stuck the yearbook under my nose.

"Show me which girls you dated."

"I didn't really date all that much."

"Don't feed me that bull, Walt Williams! Beta Club president! Cute flattop! Come on!"

"Most of the girls were hung up on the jocks. I was a nerd."

"Walt!"

"Okay! Hand me the book."

I thumbed through the pages.

"Let's see --- Irma Turnbull --- Gladys Finch --- Martha Woodstock --- Lorena Jenkins."

"I knew it. You weren't exactly a monk, were you?"

"I think this is the part where I plead the fifth."

"Oh, Walt! I'm not jealous --- just curious. I just want to know more about the guy I'm spending the rest of my life with."

Thankfully, by that time, I was dressed and it was time to go.

We walked into the Pancake House and a waitress directed us to a private room in the back.

I looked around the room and turned to Maggie.

"There must be another room somewhere. This couldn't be my class. These people are all old."

Maggie just grinned. "Have you looked in the mirror lately? Gray hair, droopy eyelids, crow's feet."

I was about to protest when an old woman with a cane hobbled up.

"Walt Williams! I'm so glad you came."

I was at a total loss.

"It's me, Wanda --- Wanda Pringle --- well, it's Bodenhammer now."

My last memory of Wanda was of her spiking the ball on the girl's volleyball team.

She grabbed me by the arm and pushed me into the room. "Look everyone! It's Walt!"

People turned and waved, and I swear, I didn't recognize a single one.

A chubby gal with bright red, obviously dyed hair, came over and put her arm around my waist.

"Hi Walt. Don't recognize me, do you?"

I smiled and shrugged.

"Gladys --- Gladys Finch." She gave Maggie the once-over.

Maggie jumped right in. "I'm Maggie, Walt's *wife*. Nice to meet you Gladys."

I noticed that she emphasized the 'wife' part.

"So you're the one that finally landed Polk's most eligible bachelor. Congratulations!" Then she turned back to me. "Remember that night after the homecoming game ---?"

Thankfully, at that moment, Wanda called the meeting to order.

"Let's all take our seats. We have a lot to discuss."

As we sat down, Maggie whispered in my ear, "I can't wait to hear about the homecoming game."

This reunion thing was just beginning and I was already regretting it.

Wanda was always a rah-rah gal. She had been one of the spark plugs of the Pep Club. It was obvious from the way she took charge of the meeting that her physical impairments hadn't dampened her enthusiasm a bit.

She opened a big loose-leaf notebook and started rattling off the various committees that would be needed to pull off the reunion. Those of us attending were supposed to volunteer our time and talents to one or more of the committees.

If there had been any way that I could have opted out for a root canal instead, I probably would have done it.

I shuddered when one of the first committees mentioned was 'decorating'. I was Junior Class President, and it was the responsibility of the Junior Class to decorate the gymnasium for the Junior-Senior Prom. I strung enough crepe paper that week to last a lifetime.

I sat as quietly and unobtrusively as possible as the committees were named. Nothing she had mentioned was even remotely within my area of expertise.

Finally, she said, "We have one more job. Over the fifty years we have lost track of many of our classmates. We need someone to try to track down as many as possible."

"Hmmm, missing persons! Right up my alley --- and if I couldn't find somebody, who would really know?"

I raised my hand. "I'll take that!"

"Thank you, Walt. Oh, and I remember what a fantastic job you did with the Junior-Senior Prom. I'll bet you'd love to help out the decorating committee!"

I felt like I had been punched in the stomach.

Everyone was looking at me expectantly.

"Uhhh --- sure. Why not?"

After the meeting, Benny Beemer tapped me

on the shoulder.

"Hey, Walt. Plant any trees lately?"

Benny was a football jock and I always suspected he had a hand in cutting down the Beta tree.

"No, Benny. Cut anything down lately?"

He smirked and walked off.

I could see that my fifty-year class reunion was going to be a real doozey!

Frank, Ernie and Paddy had gathered around the table in Ernie's apartment.

"We know that the two cops checked out the warehouse the day we left them the note because we followed them, but so far, nothing's come from it," Frank said with disgust.

"Remember, Frank," Ernie said, trying to sooth his friend, "these things take time. They probably have the place under surveillance and are looking for evidence."

"Well I'm tired of sitting around waiting for something to happen. I think it's time we took a more active part in this thing."

"Oh, really?" Paddy asked. "And just what would you have us do? Maybe storm the warehouse?"

"Sarcasm, Padre? Did you learn that in divinity school? Actually, I think we should do some surveillance of our own. We're always hearing about the shortage of manpower in the police department. I'll bet they don't have enough men to watch the place 24/7, but we could."

"Do you realize what you're saying?" Ernie said in disbelief. "That's three eight-hour shifts! One of them all night long!"

"So what have we got to do that's more important? Play bingo with Minnie Potter? And besides, none of us sleep through the night anyway. I've seen your light on at three in the morning, Ernie."

"What do you expect to accomplish?" Paddy asked.

"If that warehouse is really where the mules are unloading their drugs, we have to get proof --- see who's coming and going --- get license plates --- anything to get the cops off dead center. I figure one of us could do eight to four, the next one four to midnight and the last one midnight to eight. I'll even volunteer for the midnight to eight."

"You're really serious about this, aren't you?" Ernie asked.

"You bet I am. When I think about what Paddy said those goons are doing to those poor girls, it makes my blood boil. We may be old and worn out, but we're not dead yet. I want to do something to make a difference before I go."

Paddy looked at Ernie. "I'm in. What about you?"

"I'll take the first shift," Ernie said. "Paddy, if

you still have any influence with the Man Upstairs, you might put in a good word for us. We're going to need it."

At midnight, Frank tapped Ernie on the shoulder.

"Holy Crap!" Ernie exclaimed. "Don't sneak up on a guy like that!"

"Sorry! Anything going on?"

"A produce truck unloaded some crates about six o'clock, but it's been quiet as a mouse since then."

"Go home and get some shut-eye. We'll talk tomorrow."

As Frank sat in the darkness, he felt his senses come alive. Not far away, he heard the whistle of a train and felt the ground vibrate as it carried its load to some distant destination.

When the train had passed, he heard something rustling a few feet away. He clicked on his flashlight and the beam reflected in the eyes of a rat that had been foraging for scraps of food. He watched as the rodent lifted its head, sniffed the air and twitched his whiskers. Sensing that something wasn't quite right, it turned and scurried away.

Just past three in the morning, Frank saw headlights approaching. He crouched low and watched as three men climbed out of a panel van.

Two of the men opened the rear door of the

van while the third man opened the door to the warehouse.

The two men pulled something long and dark out of the van and carried it to the warehouse. In the light that was streaming through the door, Frank recognized what was being carried --- a body bag.

Once inside, the door was closed and Frank was once again surrounded by darkness.

"This is exactly what we've been looking for!" Frank thought. *"I've got to get in there and see what's going on!"*

Frank slipped from his hiding place and approached the warehouse door. He placed his ear against the door and heard voices.

"Can't go in here," he thought. *"Must be another way in."*

He followed the wall to another door he had seen fifty feet from the one that the men had entered.

He placed his ear against the door, but heard nothing.

He reached into his pocket and pulled out a lock-pick set.

"Thirty-five years as proprietor of Frank's Lock and Key Service has finally paid off," he thought, smiling.

He heard the 'click' as the lock snapped open.

Quietly, he opened the door and peered in. The door had opened into a hall. At the far end, he saw lights burning. He slipped in and tiptoed to a window that opened into the lighted room.

He saw the three men gathered around the

body bag that had been placed on a gurney. One of the men unzipped the bag revealing the body of a young man.

A second man ripped open the shirt of the dead man while the third retrieved a scalpel from a set of surgical tools on a nearby shelf.

Frank watched in horror as the man with the scalpel sliced open the abdomen of the corpse. The other two men spread open the man's stomach while the third one removed bags of white powder and placed them in a tray.

When they had finished, they zipped up the bag and carried it to a trash dumpster located just inside the warehouse by an overhead door.

The bags that had been removed from the mule were washed and placed in a satchel.

When it was apparent that they were finished with their grisly work, Frank retraced his steps, slipped out the door and returned to his hiding place.

A few moments later, the three men emerged from the warehouse carrying the satchel and climbed into the van.

Stunned, Frank sat in silent shock as he watched the taillights of the van disappear in the distance.

When he had regained his composure, he tried to think about what to do next. He was certain that the van was on its way to the Sunset Drive address to deliver the cocaine to Hector Corazon. Nothing he could do about that.

There was still a desecrated body in that

warehouse. If he called the cops, would they come? They couldn't enter without a search warrant and that wouldn't happen until morning.

As he was contemplating his next move, another set of headlights came into view.

A huge garbage truck pulled up to the overhead door, two men got out of the cab and raised the door.

They pushed the dumpster into the street and attached it to the big pneumatic arms on the front of the truck.

Frank watched as the contents of the dumpster spilled into the gaping hole in the truck. One man pushed the empty dumpster back into the warehouse while the other pulled the lever that compacted the trash.

Frank made a quick decision. He ran to his car and pulled into the street behind the big truck.

He followed it across town to the landfill and watched through the chain link fence as the contents were spewed into the mound of trash waiting to be covered by a gigantic bulldozer.

He had seen enough. If this information didn't get the cops to act, nothing would!

CHAPTER 7

"What about another letter?" Ernie said, as the three friends huddled together in the early morning light.

"No time!" Frank said emphatically. "That body has already been in the landfill an hour. No telling how much more trash has been piled on top of it and eventually they compact everything and cap it with dirt. We have actual evidence. I think it's time to talk to the cops."

"I agree," Paddy said. "What Frank saw trumps anything I ever heard in confessional. I think we can tell them what we know without violating any confidences."

"Then let's do it!" Ernie said, looking at his watch. "Maybe we can get to the police station before they hit the streets."

Squad meeting had just concluded and we were gathering our gear from our lockers when Dooley stuck his head in the door.

“Hey, Batman and Robin! There’s three old dudes in the lobby that want to talk to the cops that drive car 54. That’s you isn’t it?”

Ox nodded. “What do they want? We were just on our way out.”

“Hey, I’m not your secretary. Ask them yourself. They said something about a couple of letters.”

That got Ox’s attention. “Thanks, Dooley. We’ll take it from here.”

“If these guys are the real thing,” I said, “we’d better get the Captain involved. You go meet them and I’ll get the Captain.”

The Captain got Rocky Winkler on the horn and we were all waiting in the Captain’s office when Ox entered with the three old gentlemen.

“Captain, I’d like you to meet Frank Pollard, Earnest Harding and Father Patrick O’Brian. These are the guys that have been sending us love notes.”

While the introductions were being made, I started putting the pieces of the puzzle together.

“You’ve made some pretty strong accusations,” the Captain said. “I’d like to know where you came by the information.”

“Let me take a crack at that,” I said. “Father O’Brian, until a few months ago, you were at the Sacred Heart Guadelupe Church. Am I right?”

He nodded.

“Like Father Sebastian, your replacement, you must have heard some pretty disturbing things in confessional that you could not share.”

He nodded again.

"So rather than break the confidence of the confessional, you gave us just enough information to put us onto this Corazon character and hoped that we'd take it from there."

"If that's all true, what brings you here this morning?" the Captain asked. "What's changed?"

"What's changed," Father O'Brian replied, "is that we now have concrete evidence to back up what was in those letters and we can give it to you without violating the confessional. Tell them Frank."

For the next fifteen minutes, Frank Pollard shared the incredible story of how these old guys had been shadowing the cartel and the grisly spectacle that he had just witnessed.

"One of the bags must have busted in the mule's stomach," Winkler said. "They usually pump them full of laxatives and let nature take its course." He turned to Frank. "You're sure that the body is in the landfill?"

"Absolutely! I followed the truck from the warehouse to the Southeast Landfill on Indiana and watched them dump their load."

"Captain Short," Winkler said, "wouldn't you agree that with this information we have enough to get a search warrant for that warehouse?"

The Captain nodded.

"Good! Then if you'll get the paperwork started for the warrant, I'll take some men to the landfill and see if we can find that body bag. Walt, Ox, why don't you get a written statement and contact information from these gentlemen?"

"Sure thing," Ox replied.

Then Winkler turned to the three octogenarians. "Gentlemen, we really appreciate what you have done to this point and the information you have given us. Let us handle it from here. As you have seen, these men are extremely dangerous. We don't want you putting yourselves in any further danger. Understand?"

"I guess you're telling us to back off!" Frank said, with disgust.

"Exactly! When we are finally ready to make a move on these guys, we don't want any civilians in harm's way."

"Or in your way!" Frank replied, sarcastically.

"Yes, that too. I'm glad you understand. Well let's get to it."

We led the three to a conference room, took their statement and their contact information at the Whispering Hills Retirement Village.

When we were finished, Frank asked, "So what happens now?"

"That's up to Sergeant Winkler," Ox replied. "He's in charge of the drug task force. He's a good man. He'll handle it from here."

"I understand that he wants us out of the way," Paddy said, "but we have a big stake in this thing. Will you promise to let us know what's happening --- to keep us informed?"

"We'll do the best we can. We're just a

couple of grunts. Sometimes we don't know everything that's going on ourselves, but we'll try. I have your numbers."

"We appreciate it," Ernie said as they left the room.

When they were out of earshot, I said, "Three bumbling guys taking on a Mexican bandito. Reminds me of *The Three Amigos*."

"The three what?" Ox asked.

"You've never seen the movie?"

"What movie?"

"Never mind!"

It was Saturday morning and I was looking forward to a day off.

Maggie had a listing appointment scheduled for early afternoon and when she was finished with that, I had been informed that she was planning to cash in on one of the dinners out that I owed her for the Burrito Bandito debacle.

I had just polished off my coffee and Wheaties, the Breakfast of Champions, and was heading out to the front sidewalk to pick up the morning paper.

As luck would have it, Jerry collared me before I could get back to my apartment.

"Walt, what are you doing this morning?"

I held up the newspaper, but before I could declare my attentions, he forged ahead.

"If you don't have anything pressing, would you play Wii with me?"

I had no idea what he was talking about. The last time I had played wee with anyone was in the third grade when some buddies and I wrote our names in the snow.

"You want me to do what?"

"Play Wii! It's a video game."

I had seen ads on TV for some of these games, but being an old fart that could barely navigate the complexities of his cell phone, I had dismissed them as technology beyond my comprehension.

"Gee, I don't know, Jerry," I said, clutching my paper.

"Please! It's REALLY fun! I know you'll like it."

He gave me his sad puppy eyes and I caved.

"Okay, but just for a little while."

He led me into his living room and sat me down in front of his TV to which he had connected a box of some sort.

He handed me a steering wheel that had a thing in the middle full of buttons.

"We're going to play Mario Cart. It's a race game. I'll show you how it works."

For the next fifteen minutes, he explained the intricacies of the steering wheel and the functions of all of the little buttons, then he ran a few races solo to show the game in action.

"Okay, I think you're ready. I'll be Mario and

you can be Luigi. We race each other and ten other characters."

We started the game and I had just driven around the first bend when he launched a bomb at me and blew up my car.

"Hey, I thought this was a race?"

"It is, but part of winning is eliminating your opponents."

I started again, and some big monkey in another car ran over me and squashed me flat.

"That's Donkey Kong. He's a mean dude."

After being repeatedly blown up, run off the road and squashed by Jerry and other assorted creatures, I started getting the hang of it.

Soon, I was doing some bombing and squashing of my own. I learned to press on the accelerator button, crash into the rear end of the guy in front of me and push him into oblivion.

The plastic steering wheel was just like a real steering wheel and I found myself banking into curves, skidding around corners and leaping off ramps.

I looked at my watch and was shocked to see that it was almost noon.

"Hey, we'd better break for lunch."

"Why don't we have lunch at Mel's, then we can stop by Games Galore. They have all kinds of cool stuff."

He had me at Mel's Diner.

After a chicken-fried steak with mashed potatoes covered with white cream gravy, we headed to Games Galore.

When we entered, a boy with a serious acne problem greeted us.

"H-H-Hi Jerry."

My friend was already on a first name basis with the clerk.

"Hi, Warren. This is my friend, Walt. We're going to look at some of your Wii games."

"W-W-We just got some new stuff in this morning. L-L-Let me show you."

For the next ten minutes, Warren demonstrated the new games.

I had noticed a couple of other high school boys playing on a different console.

"What are they playing?" I asked.

"T-T-They're on X-Box and Play Station Three. They're into the m-m-more graphic stuff."

I watched the screen and was appalled to see a character grab another character from behind and slit his throat. Blood spewed out of the severed artery. The victim slumped to the ground and the character was on to his next kill.

"Jesus, Warren! Do kids really play this stuff?"

"T-T-That's just one game. There's a d-d-dozen others just like it or worse. It's our m-m-most popular stuff."

The phone rang and Warren went to answer it.

While he was on the line, the boys playing the blood and gore game walked up to the counter.

"Hey, pizza face! Get over here and check us

out!"

Warren dutifully rang up the sale, but it was obvious the two boys were intent on giving him a hard time.

As they were leaving, two good-looking girls walked in.

One of the jerks shouted back over his shoulder, "Hey, Marcie. Warren is lookin' for a date this weekend. Are you interested?"

The kid left laughing and Marcie and her friend did the fake finger down the throat gesture.

It was obvious that Warren was mortified.

Jerry tried to smooth things over.

"Hey, Warren. Thanks for helping us out. See you next time."

When we were back in the car, I said, "How can kids be so cruel?"

"Beats me. I guess they think it's cool to put other kids down. Are you ready for another race?"

We resumed our Mario Cart warfare and as before, I completely lost track of time. I had just blown Bowser to smithereens and knocked Jerry off the road when my cell phone vibrated.

I looked at my watch.

"Oh, crap! Maggie!"

"Uhhh, hello."

"Walt, where are you? Did you remember that we have a date?"

"I'm at Jerry's. Of course I didn't forget. I'll be right there."

I really didn't forget. I just got so involved in

that goofy game, I lost track of time.

I hurriedly showered and dressed and found Maggie pacing the floor.

"What were you two up to?"

"We were Wii-ing together."

She gave me the 'I don't believe what I'm hearing' look.

"I'll explain in the car. Let's go."

I pulled out into traffic and gave Maggie a sideways glance.

"Where to, my love," I said, trying to smooth things over. "Anyplace you like. Nothing is too good for my girl."

"Can it, Walt. You're in the doghouse and you know it! Hereford House. It's going to cost you a filet to get back in my good graces --- and what's with this weeing?"

Just then, the driver in the next lane swerved into my lane and cut me off. I didn't think --- I just reacted. I stomped on the accelerator, swerved into the next lane and as I passed him, I shook my fist and cut in to the lane in front of him.

Maggie grabbed the armrest with one hand and my leg with the other.

"WALT! What are you doing? You don't drive like that!"

Maggie's fingernails digging into my thigh brought me back into the moment. I looked in the rear view mirror and noticed that the guy I had cut off looked like a linebacker for the Kansas City Chiefs.

"Oh crap!" I said. "Hang on!"

I swerved onto a side street and as the guy whizzed by, I noticed that he was giving me the finger.

Maggie stared at me in disbelief.

"What's going on? I've never seen you like this."

"I don't remember ever being like this ----." Then it dawned on me. "Not until today!"

As we sat in the Domino's Pizza parking lot, I told Maggie the story of my adventures with Jerry, Mario, Luigi, Bowser and all the other characters I had run off the road.

When I was finished, she just shook her head in amazement and disbelief.

"That's it! No more play dates with Jerry!"

I didn't need any convincing.

As we drove to the restaurant, I thought about how that seemingly harmless game had affected me, and then I thought about the kid that was slitting throats on the other video game and wondered what he was doing tonight.

CHAPTER 8

Ox and I were anxious to hear what had transpired over the weekend with the drug cartel. After squad meeting we cornered the Captain in his office.

"Did they find the body?" Ox asked.

"Sit down, boys," the Captain said gravely.

In my experience, it's rarely good news when someone asks you to hear it sitting down. This was no exception.

"By the time Sergeant Winkler and his men arrived at the landfill, the trash had already been compacted and covered with dirt. He considered shutting down the landfill and bringing in digging equipment, but trash trucks were already lined up for a block waiting to dump. It would have taken hours to get the right equipment in there and no telling how many more hours digging and searching. It would have brought the cities rubbish removal system to a halt. He couldn't make that decision on his own, so he called the mayor. The mayor was reluctant to cause such chaos based on something an old man MIGHT have seen. So no ---- no body."

"I hope you had better results with the warrant on the warehouse," I said.

"I'm afraid not. We got the warrant all right, but somebody at the landfill must have tipped off Corazon. When we searched the warehouse, all we found were fruits and vegetables. No gurneys --- no surgical equipment."

"So we're back to square one!" Ox said, shaking his head.

"It looks that way," the Captain replied. "Sergeant Winkler will be watching both the warehouse and the Sunset Drive address, but unless something breaks soon, he'll have to re-assign his men. He has a lot of territory to cover."

"Is there anything that we can do?" I asked.

The Captain thought for a moment. "Yes, as a matter of fact there is. I've been thinking about our letter-writing friends. They're knee deep in this thing and when they hear that we struck out, they'll probably feel like they have to get involved again. I can't have three retirement home residents getting whacked by a drug lord. See what you can do to keep them calm and out of the picture. You're almost their age, so maybe you can talk some sense into them."

Actually, they were at least fifteen years older than me, but I could see his point. Age isn't necessarily a deterrent. In fact, I had discovered, by watching my own father, that when one recognizes that he is nearing the end, caution is sometimes thrown out the window. I vividly recalled the day I was summoned to the Liberty Memorial where Dad and Bernice were in handcuffs for doing the nasty at the top of the Memorial. Their only excuse --- it was on their bucket list.

"Sounds like we need to make a stop at Whispering Hills," Ox said as we headed to the cruiser.

I called Frank and ask him to get the Three Amigos together for an update. He said they'd be waiting for us.

I had driven by Whispering Hills many times, but I had not been inside. It was a beautiful facility. Since we were nearing that special age, Maggie and I had received several mailings from them attempting to lure us in with their game room, weekly tea dances and wine and cheese parties. There were small cottages for those who were ambulatory and able to take care of themselves, but when the day came that was no longer possible, the total care facility was just steps away.

Frank and his friends lived in the little cottages.

We knocked and Frank opened the door with a big smile. "Come on in. I hope you have good news for us. We've been watching the TV all weekend for some big announcement. I guess the drug boys wanted to get things wrapped up in a big bow before holding a news conference."

I hated what we had to do.

You could just see the disappointment on their faces and their jubilation turning to despair as we shared what the Captain had told us.

"So --- so what now?" Ernie asked. "Are these thugs going to get away scot-free?"

"Not at all," Ox replied. "With the information that you have given us, the Drug Task Force will be watching them closely. They'll make a mistake --- they always do, and our guys will be right there to take them down."

"I just wonder how many poor souls will die or be disfigured for life before that mistake happens?" Paddy asked, sadly.

"The Captain wanted us to thank you for what you have contributed to this investigation," Ox said, "and to remind you how dangerous these men are. You saw that for yourself, Frank. Let the department handle this from here. No one wants to see you get hurt. We promise that we'll keep you informed of our progress."

"Not a problem, officer," Frank said, getting to his feet. "I'm just sorry things didn't work out this time, but like the Canadian Mounties, I know you'll get your man --- eventually. Now if you'll excuse us, we have Bingo at ten o'clock. Minnie Potter is saving a seat for me. Who knows --- I might get lucky --- at Bingo that is."

He gave us a wink and ushered us to the door. "Thanks for coming by."

On the way back to the cruiser, Ox asked, "Did we just get the bum's rush?"

"That was exactly my thought," I replied. "I'm thinking we haven't seen the last of the Three Amigos."

"Who are these Amigo guys you keep talking about?"

"Get in the car and drive. I'll introduce you to an American comedy classic!"

After the cruiser had pulled away, Ernie said, "You took that pretty well, Frank. I'm surprised."

"The hell I did! I'm so mad I can hardly see straight. We handed that cartel to them on a silver platter and they blew it! Now we're going to have to take care of this ourselves."

"But you told the officers ---!" Paddy said.

"What did you expect me to say, Paddy? If they had an inkling that we'd be getting involved again, they'd be watching us closer than those druggies. No, we'll let things cool down a day or two before we do our thing."

"And just what 'thing' is that?" Ernie asked.

"I'm not sure yet, but I'll come up with something. You can count on it!"

Father O'Brian crossed himself.

On the way home that evening, my mind was filled with pleasant thoughts --- I envisioned a quiet dinner with my sweetie, then curling up in our recliner love seat to watch our favorite TV shows.

When I walked in the door, I got a rude

awakening --- I smelled soy sauce!

"Maggie! Do I smell ---- Chinese?"

I never was a fan of Chinese food, but after my very first day on the force, when I was hit in the chest by a box of chow mien thrown by a greasy slob, I liked it even less.

Maggie planted a kiss on my cheek. "Yes, I picked up some cashew chicken on the way home. I knew you wouldn't want to waste any time before you got started."

I drew a blank. What had I forgotten this time? "Started? Start what?"

"Your committee assignment, silly. You're Missing Persons. Remember?"

I hadn't actually forgotten. I just didn't want to remember.

"Tonight? I was hoping for ---."

"If not tonight, then when? I know you, Walt Williams. You'll put this off until the last minute. That's why you have me --- to make sure you don't do that."

I could see that I was fighting a losing battle.

"But Chinese!"

"Sit down. Everything's ready."

I sat and there were two chopsticks beside my plate.

"Give me a fork or the deal's off!"

After a less than satisfying dinner, I went to the office, plopped down in my computer chair and opened the envelope that contained the names of my missing classmates.

There were twenty-two names and I didn't remember half of them. I pulled my yearbook out of the dusty box and looked up each of their pictures. Slowly but surely I started to remember details about these apparitions from my distant past.

I figured that the best place to start was Google. Only four of them were noteworthy enough to merit a spot on the popular search engine.

I clicked on a link that said, 'Free People Search'. It took me to a website called PeopleFinder.com. I typed in the first name and 'Bingo', the person that I wanted popped up on the screen. The catch was that if I wanted to know where they lived and their phone number, it would cost me ninety-five cents. So much for 'free'.

By the time I went through my list, I had seventeen bucks invested.

An hour into my search, Maggie came in with a glass of Arbor Mist.

"How's my detective doing? Figured you could use a pick-me-up."

"Smashing!" I said. "Out of the twenty-two, it seems that twelve of them have passed beyond the veil, four of them are out of the country, two told me they could care less about the reunion and three were actually glad that I found them. I have one name left and I've been dreading it.

"Archibald Sanders."

"Why are you dreading that one?"

"Because I don't like the guy, that's why."

"Sounds like there's a story there."

"I don't want to get into it."

"Spill it!"

I could see that I was doomed.

"It was our senior year. I was dating Martha Woodstock."

"I remember you showing me her picture. Pretty girl."

"Anyway, it was time for the spring play. Archibald, or Archie, as everyone called him, was the class thespian. Some kids were athletes, some were musicians. Archie was our actor.

"The play that year was *The Adventures of Tom Sawyer*, and naturally, Archie got the male lead. Against my wishes, Martha auditioned for the part of Becky Thatcher and got it. In the play, Tom and Becky kiss, and I have to admit --- I was jealous. Every day after school for a month, they rehearsed and kissed. By the time the play was over, Martha had fallen for Archie and I got dumped. So there it is! That's why I hate Archie's guts!"

"Goodness, Walt! Some wounds heal slowly. It's been fifty years."

"I know. Stupid, isn't it?"

"So are you going to call him?"

"I suppose I have to. It's my duty."

I dialed the number that had cost me ninety-five cents and after three rings, he picked up.

"Archibald here."

"Hi Archie. This is Walt Williams." There was a long pause. "From Polk High School."

"Walter, of course. How long has it been? So

good to hear from you."

"Actually, it's been fifty years. That's why I'm calling."

In the next few minutes, I shared with him the details of the upcoming class reunion.

"So, just a couple of weeks away. Let me check on something." I heard the rustle of some papers. "Splendid! I'll actually be in Kansas City. I'm touring with the stage play, *The Game's Afoot*. I'm the understudy for the male lead who plays Sherlock Holmes. We'll be opening soon at The New Theatre Restaurant."

"So still acting after all these years."

"I'm afraid it's in the blood old chap. By any chance are you married?"

"Why yes, a couple of years now. Why do you ask?"

"Then I would love for you and your better half to be my guests on opening night. I'll leave tickets to my table at Will Call. It will be good to see you and our classmates again. Actually, I'll leave four tickets. Bring some friends. We're trying to spread the word about our show. Well, cheerio!"

Maggie had been listening to our conversation.

"Doesn't sound like Archie's holding a grudge."

"Well of course not. He got the girl!"

"Well now you have one," she said running her fingers through my hair. "Who would you rather spend the rest of this evening with? Me or Martha

Woodstock?
“Martha who?”

CHAPTER 9

"Okay, Padre, time to get to work," Frank said to his old friend.

"Just what did you have in mind?"

"You were the priest in that parish for thirty years. I know that you know who the movers and shakers are in the Latino community. It's time to pay them a visit."

"I don't know ----."

"We won't be doing anything to spill the beans about what you heard in confessional. Just a kindly old priest making a social visit."

Paddy thought for a moment. "Luis Mendoza. If anyone knows what's going on, it would be Luis, but I don't know if he will talk to us."

"Only one way to find out," Frank said, getting to his feet. "Fire up your old Buick, Ernie. I'm out of gas."

As they were heading out the door, Frank stumbled, but caught himself on the doorjamb.

"Are you okay?" Ernie asked, concern in his voice.

"Yeah, just sat too long. Gotta keep the old joints moving."

The three pulled up in front of the Mendoza home on Jarboe.

"Let me handle this," Paddy said. "This is a very tight-knit community and strangers are not always welcomed with open arms --- plus --- well, Frank, you can be a bit pushy sometimes."

Frank held up his hands in mock defense. "Your show, Paddy."

A swarthy Latino man in his mid-fifties with coal-black hair graying at the temples answered the door on the third knock.

"Father O'Brian! What a surprise! What brings you to our home?"

"Luis, good to see you again. These are my friends, Frank and Ernie. I wonder if we could have a moment of your time?"

"Certainly, Father. What is the purpose of your visit?"

A teenage girl was in the living room busy with her IPAD.

"Maybe it would be better if we could talk alone," Paddy said, motioning to the girl.

"Gloria, go to your room. I need to talk to Father O'Brian privately."

He watched as the girl disappeared into the back of the house. "This must be serious, Father."

"It is, Luis. I'll get right to the point. We know that Hector Corazon is recruiting young Latino women as drug mules. We have been working with the police, but we've hit a brick wall. We we're hoping that you could help us."

"Father," Mendoza said, shaking his head, "you have no idea what you're dealing with here. These are very bad men."

"Actually, I do know," Frank said, butting in. "I watched them cut open the stomach of a young man and then throw his body into a dumpster."

"How ---?"

"Never mind, how," Frank said continuing. "This guy needs to be stopped. Can you help us?"

"You have put my family in grave danger just by being here. Please leave!"

"Luis," Paddy said, "you have been a leader in this community for many years. People look up to you --- they depend on you. As long as he is doing his dirty business, no one in your community will be safe."

"He is right, Luis," a woman said, coming into the room.

"Consuela! You were listening?"

"Yes, my husband. I am tired of living in fear --- wondering who is watching when I go to the market --- wondering when this animal will come after one of our own girls. We trusted Father O'Brian for many years. If he thinks we can help, then we should try."

Luis sighed, "Rosalina Torres. She is in Mexico and is due back in Kansas City in two days."

"I know Rosalina," Paddy said. "I gave the child her first communion."

"Why would she do something like this?" Ernie asked.

"Simple," Luis said, "for the money. Her father lost his job, the family fell behind on their house payments and they are about to lose their home. Corazon promised her a thousand dollars. What are you going to do?"

"I'm not sure yet," Paddy said.

"You must not tell anyone where you got this information and you must not contact the Torres family. If Corazon finds out that we talked to you, then we are all dead."

"We will be careful, Luis. The last thing we want to do is put you and your family in danger. Thank you for helping us."

Back in the old Buick, Ernie asked, "So what are we going to do? We sure can't go after these bastards by ourselves."

"We have to go to the police," Paddy replied.

"They'll just screw it up again!" Frank said. "Like they did last time."

"So do you have a better idea, Sherlock?" Ernie asked.

"No, I guess not. Listen, I've got an appointment with Doc Johnson in an hour. We'll call those two cops that gave us their cards and have them come by right after lunch."

"Doc Johnson?" Ernie asked. "Is something wrong?"

"Naw, just routine. I'll give them a call and have them stop by at one o'clock."

We were about to stop for lunch at Denny's when my cell phone rang.

"Officer Williams!"

"Yes,"

"This is Frank Pollard --- you know --- one of the old guys that wrote the letters to you."

"Sure, Frank. What can I do for you?"

"My friends and I have some more information that might help you get a bead on Hector Corazon. I was wondering if you could stop by my place at one o'clock?"

"Frank! I thought we asked you guys to back off."

"Let me ask you something, officer. How much closer are you to bringing this guy in since the last time we talked?"

"Well ------."

"That's what I thought. Now do you want what we've got or not?"

"We'll be there at one."

"Be where?" Ox asked as I shut the lid on my phone.

"That was The Three Amigos. They claim they have another lead for us."

Ox laughed. "After you told me about that movie, I stopped by Blockbuster and rented it. You were right. It's a blast! I loved the part where they do their little macho thing:

Wherever there is injustice you will find us
Wherever there is suffering, we'll be there
Wherever liberty is threatened, you will find
The Three Amigos!

"Then they do that goofy thing where they slap their chest, turn their heads and cough. We should work up something like that."

"Yeah, right. I'm sure that would go over well in the squad room. I'm worried about these guys. This isn't a movie and Hector Corazon isn't El Guapo. If they keep poking around, they're going to get hurt."

Precisely at one o'clock, we knocked on Frank's door.

"Come in, officers. Let's get down to business."

In the next fifteen minutes, they told us the information that they had learned from Luis Mendoza.

"So are you sure that this Rosalina Torres will be coming back to Kansas City day after tomorrow?" Ox asked.

"That's what Luis said," Paddy replied.

"Do you know what flight?"

"No, we don't know that!" Frank said

indignantly. "How many flights can there be coming from Mexico in one day?"

"Take it easy, Frank," Ernie said.

"Do you have a photo of Rosalina?" I asked.

"No," Paddy replied. "Luis asked us not to contact the Torres family for safety reasons, but I can give you a description of her. She's --- ummm --- shall I say, plump. She's always been pretty well endowed --- up here," he said pointing to his chest. "I suppose that's why she was a good candidate for Corazon."

"Thanks a lot guys," I said, rising to leave. "We'll get this information to the drug squad. They'll know what to do."

"I certainly hope they do better than the last time!" Frank said.

"We'll keep you informed," I replied.

I called the Captain and by the time we arrived back at the precinct, he and Rocky Winkler were waiting for us.

After sharing our tip from the old guys, Winkler said, "This might just be the break we've been waiting for. Here's the plan. The passengers from all flights originating in other countries have to pass through customs. We'll get a list of the flights from Mexico arriving that day. We'll have men undercover at customs to identify this Torres girl.

When her contact picks her up, we'll follow them to that warehouse, or wherever they plan to remove the drugs and we'll have them. Captain Short, could you spare a couple of men to help us at customs --- oh, yes, we should probably have a female officer there too."

The Captain looked at us, "How about it, guys? Are you up for an undercover assignment?"

"Sure," Ox said.

"Good! Take Judy with you, too. We'll make it a family affair."

On the morning of our assignment, we had just changed into our 'Customs clothing' when Officer Dooley popped in the locker room.

"I heard that you guys were on hooter patrol. You guys get all the good stuff. A whole day just checking out women's chesticles. If you were English cops, you would be Booby Bobbies --- get it? Knocker watchers!"

"Dooley, don't you have somewhere to be?" Ox said with disgust.

Dooley got off a parting shot as he headed out the door. "Headlight hunters!"

Even though we had a description of Rosalina Torres, Rocky Winkler had told us to keep an eye out for any other suspicious mammaries. Corazon could have had more than one mule coming back packing cocaine.

"I've really been dreading this," Ox said.

"Why? This is a piece of cake compared to some of the other undercover assignments that we've had."

"Well think about it," Ox replied. "All that stuff that Dooley was talking about --- I've got to do it with my wife. Would you want to spend the day ogling women's breasts with Maggie tagging along?"

He had a point.

We picked up Judy and headed to the airport.

There were five incoming flights from Mexico City that day. They were spread far enough apart that we could be at the gate of each flight as the passengers deplaned.

Members of the drug squad were just outside each terminal ready to follow Torres and her driver after we had spotted them.

It soon became apparent that Ox and I probably weren't the best candidates for this assignment.

While I had always been an ardent admirer of women's breasts, I discovered that my method of classification lacked some finesse. 'Hmmm', 'Okay', and 'Wow!' didn't prove to be very helpful.

At least what we were to concentrate on were the 'Wow's!' We quickly discovered that neither Ox nor I could distinguish between a natural 'Wow' and a store bought 'Wow'.

Judy finally took over. "Okay, dumb asses, I'll handle this."

We stood idly by, watching Judy for a signal that something was amiss, but it never came.

When all of the passengers from the last flight from Mexico had deplaned, there had been no sign of Rosalina Torres.

"Looks like your old guys got it wrong," Judy said.

All day long, I had been watching the airport monitors for the arrival times of our Mexican flights. Dozens of flights from all over the U.S. had landed throughout the day.

I picked up the phone and called the Captain. "By any chance, did someone think to call the airlines to see if a Rosalina Torres was a ticketed passenger?"

A long silence. "No, I don't think so. We thought she would be coming from Mexico, so we covered those flights."

"Could somebody do that? I think we may have screwed up royally."

A half hour later, my cell phone rang.

"Walt, you were right. Rosalina Torres arrived at three-forty-five this afternoon on a Southwest Airlines flight from Denver."

"Damn! Corazon was one step ahead of us. Instead of booking a flight directly from Mexico to Kansas City, he booked to Denver. Torres cleared customs in Denver. Then her trip to Kansas City was just another flight for a girl returning home. We lost her!"

I was really bummed on the long drive from

the airport back to Kansas City. We had let the poor girl and her escort slip through our fingers.

I was wondering what I was going to tell Frank and his friends, when my cell phone rang again. I cringed when I saw 'Frank Pollard' pop up on my caller ID.

"Did you get her?" Frank asked expectantly.

"No, I'm sorry, we didn't."

I explained to the poor man as best as I could how we had totally botched another solid lead that he had given us.

There was a long silence when I had finished.

"Frank, are you there?"

"Yes," he said quietly, "I'm here."

"I'm so sorry ---."

"Don't worry about it," he said, cutting me off. "We'll handle it from here."

"Frank! Don't do anything stupid!"

No answer. He was gone.

Frank turned to his friends. "They blew it again. They only covered flights from Mexico. Corazon flew her into Denver and probably put her up for the night before buying her a ticket the next day. The idiots didn't bother to check."

"We put both the Mendoza and the Torres families at risk for nothing!" Paddy said.

"No, not for nothing!" Frank said

emphatically. "I'll bet they've taken the girl to the Sunset Drive House for the night. They'll probably take her to the warehouse tomorrow for the surgery, and when they do, we'll be there!"

CHAPTER 10

At daybreak, the Three Amigos had gathered at Frank's cottage.

"So what's your plan, Frank?" Ernie asked.

"We'll sit on the Sunset Drive house until we see them bring out the girl. Then we'll follow them to the warehouse or wherever they're going to extract the drugs."

"Okay, so we'll know where they're at," Paddy said, "but what then? Call the cops?"

"Not this time. If it's the warehouse, I can get into the building with my lock picks just like I did before. We'll snap some photos of the operation and THEN go to the cops --- with undisputable evidence."

"Sounds risky," Ernie said. "What if they catch us?"

"Let's just make sure that doesn't happen."

"Are you driving today, Frank?"

"No, Ernie. Let's take your old Buick again."

"But you always like to drive!"

"I'm still out of gas. Didn't have time to fill up. We'd better get rolling."

The sun was just above the treetops when they saw two men escort Rosalina Torres from the Sunset Drive mansion into a waiting SUV.

"See! Told you!" Frank said jubilantly. "Don't lose them, Ernie."

They followed the SUV through downtown and into the city market area.

"They're still using the Aztec Produce warehouse," Frank said. "That's good. We can get in and out of there in a breeze."

They parked and watched until Rosalina and her escorts had disappeared inside.

"Let's give them a few minutes to get set up," Frank said. "We want to catch them in the act."

Ten minutes later, Frank checked his watch. "Okay, let's go."

Ernie and Paddy were out of the car and waiting for Frank who seemed to be having difficulty swinging his legs out of the car."

"Something the matter, Frank?" Ernie asked.

"No, just this damned arthritis. Just give me a minute."

Frank struggled out and hung onto the car for a moment. "Okay, let's do this."

They crept quietly to the second entrance that Frank had found earlier. He pulled his lock picks out of his pocket and started to work on the door, but the picks slipped from his stiff fingers.

"Damn it!"

He retrieved his picks and tried again, this time with success.

He pushed the door open just a crack and peered in. Seeing no one, he put his finger to his lips and motioned for his friends to follow him.

They crept along the hallway to the window that opened into the operating room. Rosalina Torres was lying on a gurney. The two men that had escorted her were watching a third man in a surgical gown that had just picked up a scalpel.

"This is it!" Frank said, pulling out his cell phone. "I'll snap some photos and we'll get the hell out of here."

He was just focusing for the first picture when the cell phone suddenly came to life and blasted the theme from *Rocky*, Frank's ring tone.

The three friends looked at one another in horror.

"Were you expecting a call, Frank?" Ernie said. "You never get a call."

"Oh, crap!" Frank said, fumbling to find the right button on the phone. "I forgot that Doc Johnson was going to call this morning."

Before he could silence the thing, *Rocky* blared out again.

Frank looked into the room. The men had heard the phone and were heading in their direction.

Frank made a quick decision.

"Get out of here NOW and call the cops! No questions! Just do as I say!"

His two friends hesitated.

"Go! Now! Before it's too late."

When he saw that Ernie and Paddy were

almost to the exit, he boldly headed to the doorway of the operating room and met the two drug dealers face to face.

"Say, is there a bathroom around here someplace? My teeth are floating and I really need to take a leak!"

As Paddy quietly closed the exit door, he heard one of the men say, "Take him!"

When the two men were safely back in their car, Paddy crossed himself and said, "My God! What have we done?"

"We have to get out of here," Ernie said, firing up the engine of the old Buick. "I'll drive. You call the cops!"

Squad meeting had just started when my cell phone rang.

The Captain gave me a dirty look. He doesn't like to be interrupted.

I was about to shut the thing off when I saw Patrick O'Brian's name pop up on the caller id.

"I better take this," I whispered to Ox, and slipped into the hall as unobtrusively as possible.

"Officer Williams?"

"Yes,"

"This is Father O'Brian. They have Frank!"

"Who does? Who has Frank?"

"Corazon's men. I think we've made a terrible mistake!"

In the next few minutes, Father O'Brian relayed the story of their morning's misadventures.

I was heartsick as I listened. I should have known from the tone of Frank's voice when I told him how we had botched the airport job that he wasn't about to sit still and do nothing.

"Go home!" I said emphatically. "Don't go anywhere near that warehouse. We'll take it from here. Do you understand?"

"I do and we will."

I returned to the squad room.

"Captain, I hate to interrupt, but we have an emergency!"

As succinctly as I could, I relayed Father O'Brian's conversation.

The Captain didn't hesitate. "Williams, find Rocky Winkler and tell him to get his men to that warehouse. I'll find a judge and we'll get a search warrant. As soon as we have it in hand we'll storm the place."

"I thought that you already had a warrant."

"We did, but we found nothing incriminating, so we have to start the process from the beginning."

"But by the time --- "

"I'm sorry, Walt. It's the law. You'd better get going."

An hour later Winkler and his men invaded the warehouse, warrant in hand. As before, they found only produce workers sorting fruit and vegetables.

No Frank. No Rosalina Torres. No gurney.

Father O'Brian picked up the phone and listened quietly as Officer Williams shared the bad news.

"He's dead, isn't he?" Paddy asked, already knowing the answer.

The officer, of course, tried to reassure him that they just didn't know, but in his heart, he knew that his friend was gone.

He had just hung up when Ernie walked in the door.

Paddy just shook his head.

Ernie gave a long sigh and wiped a tear from his eye.

"I know why he did it," he said. "I just came from Doc Johnson's office. He didn't want to tell me anything because of that doctor-patient confidentiality thing, but when I told him that Frank might be dead, he spilled the beans. Frank had ALS, Lou Gehrig's disease."

"That explains a lot," Paddy said, "the stiffness in his hands and legs, the fact that he actually let you drive. He must have been going downhill pretty fast."

"He must have known," Ernie said. "That's why he did what he did to save us. He chose to die a hero rather than to slowly waste away."

"We've lost a good friend," Paddy said, putting his arm around his companion. "I guess we're not the Three Amigos anymore."

CHAPTER 11

Everyone was heartsick about the disappearance of Frank Pollard and that we had let Rosalina Torres slip through our fingers.

Rocky Winkler vowed that he would step up surveillance on the cartel, but days passed with no new leads.

The disappearance of their friend must have taken the wind out of the sails of our remaining two letter writers from Whispering Hills. Father O'Brian called once to check on our progress, but otherwise they seemed to be out of the picture.

At last the day arrived when my old classmate, Archie Sanders, was coming to Kansas City for the opening of *The Game's Afoot* at The New Theatre Restaurant.

Since Archie had offered us four tickets, we invited Ox and Judy to accompany us. Naturally, Maggie and Judy were a lot more enthusiastic about the evening affair than my partner and I. In fact, Ox was rather indignant at first that he had been roped into an evening with one of my old classmates until I told him that there was a free meal involved.

Maggie dutifully researched the play and was delighted to discover that Marion Ross, Mrs. Cunningham from the 70's TV show *Happy Days*, was to be the female lead. Archie was the understudy for the male lead who played Sherlock Holmes in the opening scene.

We arrived at the theatre a half hour early and picked up our tickets at Will-Call.

We were just hanging around the lobby looking at the artwork and goofy statuettes when I felt a tap on my shoulder.

It was Martha Woodstock.

Martha had always been a pretty girl. That's one reason why I was pissed when she dumped me for Archie Sanders. Unlike many of my classmates, upon whom Father Time had taken a toll, Martha was remarkably well preserved. If fact, after having just been on hooter patrol, it didn't take a genius to determine that Martha's mammaries were definitely defying gravity by artificial means.

"M-M-M-Martha! Imagine seeing you here!"

I've never claimed to be a silver-tongued devil.

"Hello, Walter. Good to see you after all these years."

I felt a gig in my ribs and quickly recognized my cue.

"Martha, this is my wife, Maggie, and our friends, Ox and Judy."

Maggie and Martha gave each other the full head-to-toe once-over.

It's some kind of girl thing.

Martha didn't beat around the bush. "I'm so excited to see Archie again. Have you seen him?"

"No, not yet, but I'm sure we'll see him soon. We're actually sitting at his table. He left us complementary tickets."

Martha looked like I had slapped her in the face, but she recovered quickly.

"He's probably with the other cast members. I'll just drop by your table and say 'Hi' later on."

Thankfully, at that moment, the doors opened and we took our places in line to be seated.

Once seated, we picked up our menus.

Ox and I are menu-wary. This past summer, we had spent a week aboard a cruise ship being subjected to strange food that we could neither pronounce nor enjoy.

Unfortunately, the first thing that I saw was 'steamed fresh broccoli' and I feared the worst.

Ox leaned over and pointed to an item, 'baked ziti'. "Sounds like a skin condition to me. And what's with these 'half smashed potatoes'? Was it too much trouble to smash the other half?"

Naturally, Maggie and Judy picked this up with their 'wife radar' and we each got 'the look'.

Archie still hadn't arrived by the time we were to go through the serving line. I noticed that Martha Woodstock was seated on our same row, about four tables away. She had chosen the seat that looked directly at our table. Every time I glanced her way, she was staring at us intently.

Thankfully, the menu selections were much better than we expected and Ox and I both returned with full plates.

We were about to dig in when Archie arrived.

"So sorry, Walt. Cast duties and all. I'm sure you understand."

After introductions, Archie excused himself and headed to the serving line.

He had returned and was barely seated when Martha approached.

"Archie, it's been a long time --- too long."

She leaned over giving him an unobstructed view of her ample cleavage and kissed him on the cheek.

"Why, Martha," he replied, somewhat taken aback. "What a pleasant surprise."

"I wouldn't have missed the opening night of your play for anything," she gushed. "When will you actually be performing?"

"It's uncertain at this point. I'm an understudy. I perform when the lead wants a night off or, heaven forbid, is ill. I'm on standby, so to speak."

"Here's my number," she said, slipping him a piece of paper. "Please let me know when you'll be performing. I definitely want to be here."

She gave him another peck and peek and headed back to her table.

During the meal, we talked about all the trivial stuff that people talk about when they haven't seen each other for fifty years. I noticed that Martha's eyes were riveted on Archie the whole time.

At last, the plates were cleared and the lights flickered, indicating that it was close to curtain time.

"Just a word of warning," Archie said, pointing to a page in the program. "Since I'm seated with three of the city's finest, don't be alarmed in the first scene and do something rash."

I looked where he was pointing and saw 'WARNING! This show contains the sound of gunshots.'

"My character is winged in the arm. No harm done. It's all in good fun, but the gunshot is quite loud."

The lights dimmed, the curtain rose to applause, and just as Archie had predicted, just a few minutes into the scene, 'BLAM', echoed throughout the theatre.

Patrons jumped in their seats as the actor screamed, twisted and fell to the floor.

"My, my, a bit of overacting, I'm afraid," Archie muttered.

Instead of the line that was written into the script, the actress pointed to a growing splotch of red that was oozing from under the body.

"There's no blood in this scene!" Archie declared, jumping to his feet.

"He's been shot!" the actress screamed. "He's really been shot!"

I tugged on Archie's sleeve. "So this really isn't part of the play?"

"I assure you that it is not!"

Ox jumped into action. "Walt, head for the

front door and don't let anyone out of this theatre. Judy and I will cover the back entrances. Archie, call 911. Let's go!"

I jumped from my seat and sprinted to the lobby. Fortunately, a manager was there. I showed her my badge and she had the doors locked just as a wave of frightened patrons came running for the exit.

I held up my badge and tried barking out orders, but, of course, no one paid any attention to the old guy.

When they discovered that the doors were locked, I feared there might be a genuine panic and people would be trampled and hurt, but fortunately, most of the patrons were probably Social Security recipients whose trampling days were long gone.

I was finally able to restore a semblance of order and the crowd hushed in silence as a fleet of squad cars with lights flashing and sirens blaring pulled into the front drive.

Detective Blaylock ran up the front steps. I gave him a little finger wave through the glass and he just shook his head.

The manager opened one of the doors and Blaylock entered.

"Williams, why is it that whenever there's weird crap going on, you're right in the middle of it?"

All I could do was shrug my shoulders. I had no idea, but it certainly seemed to be true.

I told him what I knew and was truly thankful when he took control of the scene.

We had acted quickly, so it was assumed that

the shooter was still in the building.

No one was allowed to leave until they had been questioned. The theatre was thoroughly searched and a snub-nosed .38 was found in one of the balcony loges that were not occupied that night.

When it was all over and done, we had the weapon, but no idea who had fired it or why.

On the way home, Maggie said, “Did anyone but me notice that Martha Woodstock was not at her table when the shot was fired?”

I certainly hadn’t. My attention was focused on the carnage on the stage.

“How in the world would you have known that?”

“Haven’t you heard the old saying, ‘keep your friends close, but keep your rivals closer’?”

“Maggie! Surely you don’t ---?”

“Walt, just shut up while you’re still ahead!”

CHAPTER 12

Under normal circumstances, I'm happy when the workday is over and I can get home to my sweetie and we can enjoy a relaxing evening together.

Not today.

Instead of a nice meal and kicking back to watch my favorite TV shows, I had to hurry off to another one of those class reunion committee meetings. Even though I had completed my missing persons assignment, I feared that there were more projects waiting to be foisted off onto some poor unsuspecting soul --- like me.

I tried to stall, but Maggie knew me too well and prodded me out the door. My revenge was that I asked her to come with me. She readily agreed, probably thinking that I might veer off the path and wind up at Mel's Diner for a piece of pie.

Wanda Pringle was the consummate committee chairperson. She was organized, authoritative and wouldn't take 'no' for an answer.

After calling the meeting to order and getting reports from the various committees, she launched into the part of the evening that I had been dreading --- new assignments.

I held my breath as she doled out task after task. Finally, she came to me.

"Walt, you're on the decorating committee. I have a special job for you. Since we have a fall theme, we thought it would be nice to have some outdoor things as accent pieces --- things like corn stalks, a bale of hay or two --- maybe some cattails if you can find them --- oh yes, and pumpkins. We'll need at least a dozen --- carved. We can count on you for that, can't we?"

Everyone was looking. What else could I say but 'yes'.

Actually, when I thought about it, I got off pretty easily. Maggie and I could take a field trip and spend the day in the country, and I didn't have to screw around with crepe paper.

I thought I was home free, but a chill ran up my spine when I heard her call my name again.

"Walt, we have another surprise that's just going to be so much fun!"

"Yeah, I'll bet!" I thought.

"As you know, there's a varsity football game on the Friday night before the class reunion. I've spoken to the Pep Club sponsor and got everything cleared with the school. Our class Powder Puff Cheerleaders will be performing on the field with the Varsity Cheerleaders. Aren't you excited?"

Actually, it was more like the feeling I always get when the doctor tells me that I'm due for a colonoscopy.

In our senior year, girls from our class played the girls from the junior class in what was billed as a Powder Puff Football Game. With genders switched, and the girls dressed in pads, some genius figured out that the cheerleaders should be guys and --- you guessed it --- I was one of the Powder Puff Cheerleaders. Not one of my prouder moments.

"Gee, I don't know --- "

"Of course you will!" Wanda gushed. "I've already spoken with Don, Kenny, Loren and Gary. They're all on board and I know that you'd feel just terrible seeing them out there on the field without you."

Like I said, the woman just doesn't understand 'no'.

"He'd love to do it!" Maggie said gleefully.

I could see right away that I had made a grievous error when I got Maggie involved in the reunion committee. She was having waaaay to much fun with this.

Just when I thought that nothing could be worse than five old guys prancing around a football stadium leading dumb cheers, she called my name again.

"Walter."

I froze. *"What now? What more humiliation could she possibly heap onto me?"*

"I was visiting with Sylvia on the entertainment committee and she reminded me that two years ago, you did an Elvis impersonation at the Sprint Center and actually won second place in the contest. We just can't let that kind of celebrity in our class go untapped. We knew you would just love to do Elvis for us as part of the evening's entertainment.

Elvis was such a part of our lives back then. It would just be perfect!"

Actually, it was an undercover assignment. A citywide Elvis contest was being held in celebration of the release of a new album of Elvis' songs that had been found thirty-four years after his death. The winner of the contest was to be the feature performer on the night of the album's release. Contestants were being picked off one by one before the contest, so I was recruited to go undercover to smoke out the attacker.

No one ever expected me to get past the first round, but somehow the specter of a sixty-seven year old Elvis caught on and I actually made it to the finals.

As I recalled that night, I knew I was in trouble. It was right after that performance, in front of nineteen thousand people, I proposed to Maggie dressed as Elvis.

Before I could even open my mouth, I heard Maggie's voice a second time.

"He'd love to do it!" Maggie just couldn't resist the opportunity to relive that special moment.

I wasn't nearly as thrilled.

It was a quiet ride home.

My head was filled with images of me making a fool of myself, first on the football field and then the next night, trying to wiggle my sixty-nine year old hips onstage.

Maggie finally broke the silence. "You're upset with me, aren't you?"

"I might as well show up dressed as Ronald McDonald. I seem to be the class clown!"

"So that's it," she replied. "After all these years, you're still worried about what your classmates are going think about you. Peer pressure is a powerful thing. Let me tell you something, Walt Williams."

"What's that?" I answered, glumly.

"You have nothing to prove. Have you taken a close look at your classmates?"

"Like what?"

"A few of them are in decent shape, but many of them are using canes or walkers. Everyone I've seen so far, except Martha and her Botox, is wrinkled. Almost everyone is retired, and look at you. You're healthy, vibrant, and you go to work every day doing the job of a man thirty years younger than you.

"When you're out there on that football field acting like an old fool and when you're onstage performing, the guys in your class are going to be wishing they could do what you do and the girls are going to be wondering how they let a guy like you slip away!"

I guess I hadn't really thought about it like that.

"You really think so?"

"I know so!"

Suddenly, I felt better about the whole thing. Maggie has a way of making that happen. That's why I keep her around.

We decided that if we were going to have a day in the country, we should start with a good country breakfast, so we jumped in the car and headed to the Crackerbarrel restaurant for a plate of biscuits and gravy.

When our tummies were full, we pointed the car in an eastward direction and found ourselves on Blue Mills Road.

We had decided to just drive the rural roads until we found what we were looking for --- we weren't exactly sure what that was, but we figured that we'd know it when we saw it.

Suddenly, there it was --- a sign read, 'Straw - $5.00 a bale'.

"Sounds right to me," I said, turning up a gravel road.

There were fields on each side of the road. On one side we saw the remnants of a cornfield and a few stray stalks were still standing along the edge. On the other side, was a pasture with a small pond and at one end of the pond, cattails stood erect with their brown heads gently blowing in the breeze.

"Looks like we might be able to get everything we need right here," Maggie said. "One stop shopping!"

We drove almost a mile before we came to a farmhouse with the same 'straw' sign on the fence.

I pulled into the driveway and as soon as we

stepped out of the car, a big yellow lab trotted up to meet us.

I just stood there awaiting the inevitable. To this day I have never met a dog that could keep its nose out of my crotch.

I wasn't disappointed.

The big dog buried her snoot right between my legs, gave me a sniff and licked the back of my hand. Apparently I had passed. Naturally her drool had left a wet spot right beside my zipper.

"Looks like you and Daisy has become friends," said a voice coming from the direction of the barn.

An old guy in a straw hat and Big Smith overalls came striding up.

"You city folks lost?"

"No, actually we saw your sign. We'd like to buy two bales of your straw."

He looked us over skeptically, "What's a city feller want with straw?"

"Decoration. We're decorating for our fiftieth reunion and having a fall theme."

He spat a big wad of tobacco juice, some of which splattered on my shoe.

"Long as you got the ten bucks, I guess I don't give a rat's ass what you do with it."

"We also noticed driving in," Maggie said, "that you still have some corn stalks standing in one of your fields. We'd like to buy some of those too."

"Can't sell 'em to ya."

"Why not?" Maggie asked surprised.

"Cause it wouldn't be right. Got no corn on 'em. It's already been shucked. I can give 'em to you though."

"Thank you very much. That's very kind of you. We also noticed some cattails by your pond. Could we buy a few of those?"

"Nope! Don't sell weeds. Damn things is a nuisance. They'll take over a whole pond if'n you let 'em. Take as many as you want."

The farmer was being generous so I decided to forgive the wad of tobacco stuck to the toe of my shoe and the slime dripping from my crotch.

We paid the man and backed up to his barn. After the straw was loaded, he said, "Take care around that pond. With all the rain, the ground is kinda soggy. Don't want to have to come pull your ass out of the mud."

I had brought a couple of Willie's trimming tools and we cut the cornstalks without incident.

I pulled to the side of the road beside the pond and climbed through the fence.

"Remember what the farmer said about the mud," Maggie shouted as I approached the pond.

I walked gingerly to the edge, but the cattails were just out of reach. I tested the next step and it seemed solid enough, so I put my weight on that foot and reached for the nearest cattail.

I heard a 'SCHLOOOP!' and my foot sunk a good six inches in sticky, muddy goo. I immediately felt the cold water seeping into my shoe and reflexively lifted my leg.

My leg and my foot came easily out of the mud, but my shoe was still being held firmly in the muck and filling with water fast.

So there I was, standing on one leg like a gray-haired flamingo, holding Willie's tool in one hand while trying to keep my balance.

I tossed the tool and took a step backwards searching for solid ground. By the time I had regained my footing, my shoe was almost out of sight.

I got down on my hands and knees and fished around in the muck hole until I found my shoe. I pulled with all of my might and finally, 'SCHLOOOP!' the shoe came loose.

I emptied the water and wiped away as much mud as possible on the grass. I gritted my teeth and slipped the thing on --- not a pleasant sensation.

Maggie had witnessed the whole debacle from the road and as I sloshed back to the car, she exclaimed, "Walt, are you all right?"

"I'll be fine, but the Polk High School reunion is just going to have to survive without cattails!"

We headed back down the road and after a few hundred feet, Maggie pointed into another field. "Look hedge apples! Those are definitely fall things. Since we didn't get cattails, how about picking up a few of those. Do you think the farmer would mind?"

I was pretty sure that he wouldn't. I remembered from my days on my grandfather's farm, that the big green balls were even more of a nuisance than cattails.

"No, he won't care. I'll go grab a hand full and we'll head home before my foot shrivels up.

I crawled through the fence and headed to the big tree about a hundred feet away.

I had to walk carefully because the pasture was littered with meadow muffins. The last thing I wanted to do was step into a fresh pile of cow poop.

It took a few minutes to sort through the hedge apples that had fallen and find a half-dozen that were still in pristine condition.

My arms were finally loaded and I was about to head back to the car when I heard Maggie scream.

"Walt! Look Out!"

I looked in the direction that Maggie was pointing and fifty feet away from me, one of those big ugly bulls with a hump on its back was pawing the dirt, snorting and giving me the evil eye.

It suddenly dawned on me that meadow muffins just don't magically appear in a field out of thin air. Something put them there, and in this case, a big, mean something.

My last encounter with a bull was on my first day on the job. A perp was pointing a gun at my head, and like me, failed to notice a three thousand pound behemoth that had zeroed in on his butt.

That bull saved my hide, but this one seemed to have other ideas.

As I slowly backed away, I remembered something about dogs being able to smell fear. If it was the same with bulls, he was probably getting a snootful.

I would walk backward a few steps and he would advance a few steps. I figured that if I could keep doing that and maintain the space between us, I would soon be within sprinting distance of the fence.

Everything seemed to be working according to plan until I took a step back and landed squarely on top of a hedge ball.

Naturally, being round, the ball rolled, my feet flew into the air and I landed on my back.

While I was momentarily suspended in mid air, my fear was that I was going to land on one of those hard round hedge apples. When I didn't, there was a moment of relief until I felt a warm, sticky substance oozing into the back of my shirt and trousers, followed by a pungent odor that nearly cost me my biscuits and gravy.

I had done a back flip into one of Mr. Quarterpounder's meadow muffins.

At that moment, the term, 'Bullshit!' took on new meaning for me.

This turn of events seemed to push the bull over the edge, like maybe I had violated his sacred depository or something. He ceased pawing and started galloping. I looked over my shoulder and saw that I was maybe thirty feet from the fence.

I jumped to my feet and sprinted as fast as I could. I remembered that the shortest distance between two points is a straight line. Unfortunately, that straight line bisected a half dozen more land mines and by the time I hit the ground and wiggled under the barbed-wire fence, I was covered from head to toe with the remnants of my adversary's latest meals.

Maggie rushed to my side. She has always been quite supportive when my life has been in danger --- but not this time.

She took one look and one whiff, "AAAAAKKKK!" then sprinted twenty feet upwind.

I just stood there in shock, looking like the tar baby in *Song of the South*, only it wasn't tar that I was covered with.

"W - W - Walt," she gagged. "Get out of those clothes!"

"Right here?"

"Well you're not getting in the car like that!"

I could see her point.

I stripped down to my skivvies, but the pungent goo had soaked all the way through.

"Those too," she said.

"But Maggie! I'll be buck naked!"

"Do it," she said, handing me a blanket that we carried in the car for emergencies. This certainly qualified as an emergency in my book.

The bull, who had followed me to the fence had been watching the whole episode with great interest. I swear, I think he was smiling!

Figuring that I would get in one parting shot, I hung my clothes on the fence, fashioning them in such a way as to actually look like a man leaning against the fence. I put my poor shoes that had been hocked on, sunk in the mud and buried in poop, right under the pants legs. I hated to say goodbye. I really liked those shoes.

I thought that might give the bull something to think about for a while, and I knew for darn sure that when the farmer found my little surprise, he would have a story to tell around the cook stove that wouldn't be topped for years to come.

Even stripped naked and wrapped in a blanket, Maggie made me ride in the back seat.

It was a quiet ride home. Neither of us wanted to open our mouths or take a deep breath.

One thought that popped into my mind was that there weren't going to be any hedge balls at the reunion either. No cattails --- no hedge balls. I hoped that wouldn't be a deal breaker.

When we pulled up in front of the building, my worst fears were confirmed. Willie, Jerry and the Professor were all sitting on the front porch.

None of the three are normally at a loss for words, but the apparition that crawled out of the backseat definitely left them speechless --- until I got within smelling distance.

"Whoooowie!" Willie said. "You sho'is ripe!"

I knew that I wouldn't have a moment's peace until I had satisfied their curiosity, so I plopped down on the step and told them the whole disgusting story.

Jerry, of course, couldn't wait until I was finished. I could see him mentally sorting through his poop jokes as I was talking.

He didn't let me down.

"There are two flies sitting on a pile of poop.

When one fly farts, the other fly looks at him and says, 'Hey do ya mind? I'm eating here!'"

Wearily, I struggled to my feet, and as I was climbing the stairs, naked, wrapped in a blanket, leaving a noxious trail behind me, a thought popped into my mind. "If only my classmates could see me now!"

CHAPTER 13

Father O'Brian had just poured his first cup of coffee when there was a knock on the door.

"Just in time for a cup of joe," Paddy said, ushering his friend into the kitchen. "What's on your mind?"

"You know darn well what's on my mind and I know it's on yours too. How can we just go back to our normal lives after what's happened? How can we play Bingo when the men that murdered Frank are running around scot-free? Have you heard anything from the cops?"

"I called the old guy a few days ago, but there was nothing new. I think they're stumped. This Corazon is a slippery character."

"So what are we going to do about it?"

"What would you suggest?"

"The cops can't watch Corazon 24/7," Ernie replied. "It's a manpower issue. They're already spread thin, but you and me --- we've got plenty of time --- at least what time is left for us. I say we make the most of it. Let's sit on the guy until he makes a mistake. I'd rather spend my final days doing that than watching Oprah on TV with Minnie Potter."

Father O'Brian thought for a moment. "You're right, Ernie. When one of the Three Amigos goes down, it's up to the other two to make things right. I'm with you!"

"Great! I'll fire up the old Buick while you pour that coffee into a thermos. Maybe we'll stop by Dunkin' Donuts on the way."

Maggie was surprised to see me get up from the table before I had finished my second cup of coffee.

"What's the rush?"

"Ox is leaving his SUV at the dealership for some brake work. I'm supposed to pick him up. See you tonight."

"Try to avoid pastures today," she said as I kissed her on the cheek. "I'm not sure I can tolerate another episode like yesterday. I love you --- but there are limits."

"Very funny!"

Ox was waiting on the curb in front of the dealership. He climbed in and immediately wrinkled his nose.

"What's that smell? It reminds me of the stockyards."

I shared the story of my ill-fated encounter with Ferdinand the Bull. To his credit, Ox held it in right up to the point where I was standing naked in a farmer's field wrapped in a blanket.

"Pictures!" he said, getting all choked up. "Did Maggie get any pictures?"

"I certainly hope not!"

"That's got to be one of your best, Walt. In fact, it deserves a donut! Pull in here. I'll buy."

Apparently, the pungent aroma filling the car hadn't dampened his appetite.

I pulled into the Dunkin' Donuts parking lot just as Ernest Harding was walking out the door with a box under his arm

"Aren't those our two letter writers?" Ox asked pointing to the old Buick.

"Sure are. Wonder what they're up to?"

"Let's find out!"

Ernie had just fired up the engine when Ox tapped on the window.

"Officer! Imagine that! Seeing two cops at a donut shop."

Ox ignored the barb.

"Hi Mr. Harding, Father O'Brian. Just wanted to say how sorry we are about your missing friend."

"Thank you," Paddy replied. "Any news?"

"I'm afraid not. What are you two up to today?"

"We're --- uhh --- we're going to the museum. Heard there's a new exhibit in town.

Ox looked at the donuts and thermos. "Must be planning on spending the whole day."

"You never know. Later on we might play chess with some of the guys at Loose Park."

"Sure. Well, have a good day --- and don't do anything you might regret."

"Hey," Ernie replied, rolling up the window, "how much trouble could we get into at the museum?"

"Those guys are up to something," Ox said, as we watched them pull into the street. "I can just feel it."

"You're right. I'd bet anything that they won't be anywhere close to a museum today."

On the way to the precinct, my cell phone rang.

"Walt? This is Archie Sanders."

"Hi Archie. How are things at the theatre?"

"That's what I'm calling about. You and Maggie didn't get to see the play because of that unfortunate incident the other night and I thought you might want a second chance. We've been sold out every night and tickets have been hard to come by, but I've scored a couple for this Thursday. Think you could make it?"

Normally, our evenings are free, but as luck would have it, I had planned pumpkin carving that evening to fulfill the rest of my decorating committee duties.

"I'd love to, Archie, but I've already made a commitment. We're pumpkin carving that night. Maybe you could give them to Martha Woodstock. I'm sure she'd love another opportunity to see the play."

"No need for that, old chap. Martha has been

at almost every performance and I can't get away from the theatre without her corralling me. It's almost like I'm being stalked."

"The price of fame. Now that you're the lead, are you going to make it to the reunion?"

"Wouldn't miss it. The troupe has hired an understudy for me and he's coming along nicely. I've already asked for the evening off."

"By the way, how's your friend that was shot?"

"He's coming along nicely, but probably won't be back onstage while we're in Kansas City."

"Good to hear. Well, see you there --- and thanks for the offer of the tickets."

Ox had been listening to our conversation.

"Pumpkin carving? You're really into this reunion thing, aren't you?"

"Not by choice. Wanda Pringle, the reunion committee chairman, is like a drill sergeant, and Maggie is playing right into her hands."

"Really! How so?"

I told him about reprising my roles as a Powder Puff Cheerleader and an Elvis impersonator.

Ox almost choked on his long john. "A cheerleader! Fabulous! Normally, you couldn't get me anywhere close to a high school football game, but I wouldn't miss this one for all the donuts in Kansas City!"

I pulled into the parking garage and Detective Blaylock pulled in behind me. My recent conversation with Archie had aroused my curiosity.

"Good morning, Derek. Got a minute?"

"Sure, Walt. What's up?"

"I was just wondering about the shooting at the New Theatre Restaurant. Any leads?"

He shook his head. "Not a thing. The actor that was shot was from out of town. He seemed to be well liked by everyone in the cast. The only possible suspect that might have a motive also has an alibi."

"Who's that?"

"Your friend, Archibald Sanders, but he was sitting with you when the shooting occurred."

I was shocked. "What possible reason would Archie have to shoot the guy?"

"Money, one of the usual big four motives. He was the understudy, but with this guy out of the way, he became the lead. More money. Motive."

It was hard to believe that my old classmate would wing a fellow thespian, but what did I really know about the theatre, or about him for that matter. I hadn't seen him in fifty years.

"You said 'one of the big four'. What are the others?"

"Money, power, revenge and lust. Any time there's a crime, you can bet one of them is involved."

"Thanks, Derek. Please let me know if you get any breaks in the case."

"Will do."

Ox had been listening to our conversation.

"If your friend didn't do it for the money, there might just be another possibility."

"What's that?"

"The lust thing. After Martha Woodstock made her appearance at our table, Maggie and Judy made a trip to the powder room. Maggie might have mentioned how Martha dumped you for the actor dude in high school."

"You've got to be kidding!" I said indignantly. "Is nothing sacred?"

"Don't get your panties in a wad. It happens to all of us at one time or another. Anyway, on the way home, Judy told me that Martha was staring at Archie throughout the whole meal. The two girls concluded that Martha was still carrying a torch for the guy. Then, of course, Maggie noticed that Martha was not at her table when the shooting happened. She was conveniently in the ladies room. And now, after hearing your conversation with your friend that she is stalking the guy --- well --- put two and two together --- the lust thing"

"Martha? The shooter? But why? That's a real stretch and even if it's true, how would you ever prove it?"

"Martha and Archie are both going to be at the reunion. Right?"

"Yes,"

"And you're going to be doing your Elvis thing?"

"Unfortunately."

"Then I have an idea." He looked at his watch. "We're going to be late for squad meeting. I'll tell you later."

We slipped into our seats next to Officer

Dooley just as the Captain entered the room.

Dooley wrinkled his nose and gave us the once-over.

"What's that smell? Dudes! Did you whack a porta-potty on the way to work?"

It seemed that Ferdinand the Bull was getting the last laugh after all.

Father O'Brian and Ernie had parked inconspicuously a block from the Corazon mansion on Sunset Drive.

"Last donut, Paddy. Shall we split it?"

"No, it's all yours, Ernie. This surveillance stuff is pretty boring. Maybe we should bring a deck of cards next time. I know I can take you in gin rummy."

Ernie was about to wolf down the last cruller when the big, iron gates swung open and the black SUV pulled into the street.

He handed the cruller to Father O'Brian and started the engine. "Showtime!"

As before, they followed the SUV through the Plaza and onto Southwest Trafficway.

"Must be heading to the City Market again," Paddy said.

But instead of winding through downtown to Walnut Street and the City Market, they headed west on the Twelfth Street Viaduct.

“Nope,” Ernie said. “They’re going to the West Bottoms.”

The West Bottoms, laying in the flood plain between downtown Kansas City and the Missouri River was a hodge-podge of warehouses and industrial plants, criss-crossed by railroad tracks that serviced the loading docks.

The SUV exited onto Mulberry and headed north toward the river.

Ernie had done a good job of staying far enough back so they wouldn’t be noticed, but as they turned onto Mulberry, Ernie stepped on the gas.

“What are you doing? Paddy exclaimed, grabbing the armrest.

Ernie just pointed to a train that was approaching Mulberry.

The SUV had just cleared the tracks when the crossing arm dropped, cutting off the old Buick.

“Damn!” Ernie said. “Oh, sorry, Father.”

“No need! My sentiments exactly!”

It was a full five minutes before the train passed and the arm lifted. The SUV was nowhere in sight.

“Looks like we lost them,” Ernie said with disgust.

“Not so fast, Ernie. It’s just a few blocks to the river. They can’t have gone far. Let’s just drive around.”

They followed Mulberry all the way to the river, but saw nothing. On the way back, they turned west onto Eighth Street that led them to Hickory.

“Look!” Paddy said, pointing to a warehouse halfway down the block on Hickory. Isn’t that the SUV?”

“Sure is. Since the cops raided their other warehouse twice, they must have found a new location to do their dirty work. Probably nothing at the City Market but vegetables now.”

“So what should we do?” Paddy asked. “Call the cops?”

“And tell them what? Unless we know for sure that something is going on in there --- unless we have real proof, they’ll just raid the place, find nothing and Corazon will find a new location. No, we’ll just have to wait and watch until we know for sure.”

They pulled into a vacant lot and parked the old Buick behind a dumpster, determined to do whatever was necessary to avenge the death of their friend.

CHAPTER 14

After work on Thursday, I stopped by the supermarket and picked up a dozen pumpkins.

The idea of gutting and cutting all of those things by myself had seemed pretty daunting, so I had arranged a P-P-P Party, Pumpkins, Pizza and Peach Chardonney, Arbor Mist, of course.

I knew that the folks in my building would do most anything for a slice of pepperoni with double cheese, so recruiting able bodies for the carving committee was a breeze.

I had forgotten to include Mary in our fitness club caper and had gotten a royal butt-chewing for my negligence. I wasn't about to let that happen again, so I stopped by the Three Trails to pick her up.

She was standing by the curb holding her purse in one hand and butcher knife in the other. Given her exploits with a bat and a pistol over the past years, the tenants had developed a healthy respect and rarely ever gave her a minute's trouble. I figured that the specter of her standing there with a butcher knife did nothing to dispel that illusion.

"Hey, Mr. Walt," she said, climbing into the car. "Brought my own tool."

"I see that. Those pumpkins don't stand a chance."

Mary seemed more subdued than usual. "You know, I been thinking a lot about this reunion of yours. Fifty years --- that's pretty special --- heck, just bein' alive that long and gettin' to see old friends. I never had no reunion 'cause I never graduated from high school. After my daddy ran off, I had to quit and get a job to help support the family."

I had known Mary for many years, but I really didn't know much about her early life.

"Then momma passed on and my brother got himself killed in the war and my family just kinda disappeared. I got a sister out there somewhere, but I ain't seen her in years. Wouldn't know her if she walked onto the porch at the Three Trails."

"Gee, Mary. I'm sorry. I didn't know."

"Of course you didn't, cause I never told you. I just wanted to thank you for invitin' me tonight. You and Miss Maggie and Willie --- you're all the family I got, so it's really special to me."

On the way to the apartment, Mary's comments forced me to do some soul searching. From the very beginning, I had been grousing about getting involved in my class reunion, and Mary would have given her eyeteeth to have had one to enjoy. I had been blessed with a wonderful wife and a dad that had come back into my life after many years. I was surrounded by friends that had put their lives on the line for me more times than I wanted to think about.

Sometimes, it just takes a moment, to see your life from someone else's perspective to make you appreciate what you have.

We pulled up in front of the building at the same time as the pizza guy. I paid him, and Mary and I headed up the stairs, our arms loaded with pizza boxes.

The gang was all there, and I could almost hear them salivating as the warm, cheesy pizza smell permeated the room.

Dad and Bernice grabbed one box, Jerry and Willie grabbed a second one, and Mary teamed up with the Professor.

“Looks like it’s you and me, Babe,” I said as Maggie took the last box from my hands.

It was a delight watching this diverse group of seniors wiping grease off their mouths and washing the pizza down with huge glasses of Arbor Mist.

At one point, I wondered if I had made a mistake, filling them with alcohol just before they were to attack the pumpkins with sharp knives, but then somebody filled my own glass for a third time and I really didn’t care anymore.

When the last scrap of pizza had disappeared, I announced the inevitable. “Okay, time to get carving and earn that pizza. Every man to the car and grab a pumpkin.”

My announcement was met with a chorus of groans.

“You all go ahead,” Dad said, putting his arms around Bernice. “I’ve got my pumpkin right here.”

Bernice giggled and punched him in the arm.

With a great deal of groaning and grunting, the twelve pumpkins were finally on our kitchen table.

"Okay, how about this --- Maggie and Bernice can draw the lines on the pumpkins, Mary and the Professor can cut the tops open, Willie can scoop out the seeds ---."

"Hold on jus' a minute," Willie interrupted. "How come I gotta stick my hand in dat nasty place and pull out the seeds?"

Jerry jumped right on that one. "Because we figured that you've had your hands in more nasty places than all the rest of us put together. You're just a natural."

Willie thought about it for a moment and must have assumed that it was a compliment. "You probably right 'bout dat. I'll do it!"

"Good! When the seeds are out, the rest of us can carve the faces."

We each tackled our assignments with gusto.

Jerry was patiently waiting for his first pumpkin to carve. I could see the wheels turning in his head.

"You all want to hear a pumpkin joke?"

We all knew it didn't matter what we said. We were going to hear it one way or the other.

"One day two pumpkins, who were best friends, were walking together down the street. They stepped off the curb and a speeding car came around the corner and ran one of them over. The uninjured pumpkin called 911 and helped his injured friend as best he was able. The injured pumpkin was taken to emergency at the hospital and rushed into surgery. After a long and agonizing wait, the doctor finally appeared. He told the uninjured pumpkin, 'I have good news, and I have bad news. The good news is that your friend is going to pull through. The bad news is that he's going to be a vegetable for the rest of his life'."

"Dat's jus' sick!" Willie exclaimed.

Our normally stoic Professor must have been feeling the after effects of the Arbor Mist. "And do you know what you get when you divide the circumference of a pumpkin by its diameter?"

We all shook our heads.

"Pumpkin pi!" he said with a silly grin on his face.

When the carving was finished, I ushered our friends out the door and drove Mary home.

The next morning, in the light of day and out from under the spell of the Arbor Mist, I took a closer look at our carvings.

To say that they left something to be desired would have been an understatement. I hoped that Wanda Pringle wouldn't notice. I didn't want to lose my job.

The weekend filled with 50th reunion activities was fast approaching.

I dutifully packed our questionable jack-o-lanterns into the car to drop off to Wanda. I had been excused from the crepe paper hanging and balloon blowing since I had to spend time preparing for my appearance as Elvis.

Maggie insisted on accompanying me, mumbling something about not letting me out of her sight around *THOSE* women. I wasn't sure whether she was worried about them or me.

I had just finished unloading the pumpkins in Wanda's garage when she accosted us in the driveway.

"Exciting news! We have so many people coming from out of town that haven't been in Polk High since they graduated, and they are interested in seeing the changes to our old alma mater, so we have arranged a tour for this Friday morning. I figured that you and Maggie would want to come."

Wandering around the halls of a drafty old school building wasn't exactly high on my list of things to do.

"Gee, I don't know ---."

"Of course we'll be there," Maggie gushed. "Wouldn't miss it. What time?"

"Nine o'clock. We'll meet at the front entrance."

As she walked by our pumpkins, I saw her do a double take and shake her head. It was probably a good thing that I wouldn't be hanging any crepe paper.

I couldn't believe that I had been roped into

another activity. “A school tour? Really?”

“Quit your fussing, Walt. You’re my husband and I love you. I missed out on your early years. This reunion is my way of getting to know you better. Putting all those old yearbook photos in the actual school context makes it more real for me. You should be happy that I want to know everything there is to know about the man I married.”

How could I argue with something like that?

At nine o’clock on Friday, about thirty former students and their spouses had gathered in the front hallway of Polk High.

With the exception of the women that had been on the planning committee, I didn’t recognize a soul.

A Miss Wells from the office staff had drawn the short straw and been assigned as our tour guide.

She began by pointing out the obvious --- there had been a lot of changes in the past fifty years, remodeling, additions and, of course, the new computer lab.

Our first stop was the cafeteria. In the old days, there were huge windows along one wall that opened up into a grassy courtyard. It was in that courtyard that we had planted the ill-fated Beta Tree. That courtyard was now the site of the computer sciences building.

When I mentioned all of that to Maggie, she pointed out that it was probably just as well that the Beta Tree didn't survive. Had it lived to be a mighty oak, it would have still been chopped to make way for the new building.

Progress.

Our next stop was the gymnasium.

Not a lot of happy memories for me there. I remembered getting whacked playing dodge ball, running laps and trying unsuccessfully to climb the stupid rope with everyone watching.

All these things were running through my mind when I felt a tap on my shoulder.

"Walt? Walt Williams?"

A mountain of a guy, 6'2" and weighing a good two-eighty was towering over me.

"It's Eddie. Eddie Delaney."

"Oh, yes! Eddie Delaney, the jock, and one of the coach's pets."

"Hey, Eddie."

"Remember that time I gave you a wedgie and you were pulling your pants out of your crack when the Pep Club girls walked in?"

I remembered all right.

"Yeah, good times."

Maggie tried to keep a straight face, but it just wasn't working.

Thankfully, Miss Wells announced that it was time to move on and I was spared having to recall any more of the many embarrassing moments we nerds had suffered at the hands of the beefy goon squad.

We were in the hallway, on the way to the library when an alarm sounded and a voice blasted over the intercom system.

"CODE PURPLE! CODE PURPLE! THIS IS NOT A DRILL!"

The few students and teachers that had been in the hall immediately rushed into the closest room. Doors slammed shut, locks clicked and shades were drawn.

I saw the look of alarm on Miss Well's face.

"What's a code purple?" I asked as she frantically looked around for a place into which she could herd her elderly charges.

"Gun! There's a gun somewhere in the building. This is a complete lockdown. No one goes in or out of the building."

She decided on the hallway lavatories and was issuing orders for us to go into either the girl's or boy's bathroom, when the principal came racing down the hall.

"Good thinking, Miss Wells. Keep these people in there until we've been given the all clear."

I grabbed the principal by the arm and showed him my badge.

"My name is Walt Williams and I'm a police officer. What's happening?"

"We have a student with a handgun. He has barricaded himself in room 102. He has hostages. We've called 911 and the police are on their way."

"Take me to room 102. I can assess the situation and report to the responding officers."

The principal led the way, and thankfully, the door shade had not been pulled. I quietly peered into the room and what I saw sent cold chills through my body.

A boy had another boy on his knees and was pressing a pistol against the back of his head. Their backs were to the door and I couldn't see their faces.

Immediately, images of the mass murders at Columbine High School in Colorado and Sandy Hook School in Newton, Connecticut flooded my mind.

I backed away from the door, pulled out my cell phone and dialed 911.

"What is your emergency?"

"This is Officer Walter Williams, Badge 714. I'm inside the Polk High School and I have eyes on the gunman. Patch me through to the responding officers."

After a moment of silence, a gruff voice came on the line.

"Officer Williams, this is Commander Crowder with the First Response Team. What's the situation and why are you there?"

"I'm here on a fiftieth class reunion tour. The gunman is holding one student at gunpoint and there are another twenty students in the class. No shots have been fired yet and, so far, no injuries or fatalities."

"Are there external windows into the

classroom?"

I peeked into the room again.

"Yes, sir. A bank of windows on the front of the building facing south."

"We're still at least ten minutes away. Are you carrying your off-duty weapon?"

Much to the chagrin of my partner and my captain, I had never felt comfortable packing heat when I wasn't actually on duty.

"No sir, I'm not."

"Fantastic! I certainly hope the gunman doesn't start firing before we arrive. This is exactly why officers carry off-duty weapons!"

"Yes, sir."

It was probably just as well that I was not armed. I wasn't sure that I could have shot a young boy.

"Keep your eyes on the situation and let me know if anything changes."

I crept back to the door and peeked in. Nothing had changed but it was obvious that the gunman was struggling with his emotions.

A few minutes later, I saw the First Response Team pull up in into the school parking lot. Officers surrounded the school and snipers set up opposite the bank of windows.

The gunman had seen the police arrive and that seemed to agitate him even more. He turned and glanced at the door and I saw his face for the first time.

It was Warren, the pizza-faced kid from

Games Galore, and the boy on his knees was the kid that had been heckling him at the store.

Commander Crowder's voice crackled over my cell phone.

"Williams, are you still there? What's the situation?"

"Pretty much the same, Commander, except the boy became quite agitated when he saw your men deploy."

"We have him in our crosshairs. The negotiating team will arrive shortly. I just hope he doesn't start shooting before they arrive. If he pulls that trigger, we'll drop him before he can fire a second round."

I could imagine an armor-piercing shell shattering the window and Warren's head exploding like a ripe melon.

"Commander, I know that boy. He's not crazy or deranged. He's just a confused kid. I'd like to talk to him."

"Not a chance! You have no hostage negotiating training. You might just set him off."

"That could be, but a friendly face from someone he knows might just calm him down."

"Williams! ---"

I knew I was fighting a losing battle with the Commander and in most situations, he was probably right, but I couldn't just stand by and let the kid get shot.

I snapped my phone shut before he could order me to stand down.

I crept back to the door and gently tapped.

Warren whirled and pointed the gun at the door.

"G-G-Go away! I'll shoot!"

"Warren, it's me, Walt Williams. I met you a couple of weeks ago at Games Galore. I came in with your friend, Jerry, and you showed us some new Wii games. Remember?"

I could see him trying to remember.

"W-W-What do you want. What are you d- d-doing here?"

"Actually, I'm here on a school tour. I guess you're kind of a detour. Can we talk?"

He thought for a moment. "N-N-Nothing to talk about. G-G-Go away!"

"Warren, I think we do have something to talk about. You see, I know exactly how you're feeling right now."

He looked confused. "How c-c-could you know how I feel?"

"Because I was a nerd in high school too. I know how it feels for the jocks and the cool guys to pick on you. Am I right?"

He didn't answer.

"Warren, I'm coming in now so that we can talk more. I'm not armed. There are no cops with me. I just want to talk --- you and me."

He didn't object, so I slowly pushed the door open.

He backed away when I entered, but I could tell that he recognized me.

"Warren, I'm here because it's my fiftieth class reunion."

"S-S-So what? What's that got to d- d-do with me?"

"It's what I've learned after being away from this place for fifty years. When I was here, I was at the mercy of the jocks, just like you. I was Beta Club president and we planted a tree right out there in the courtyard where the Computer Science building is now. You know what the idiots did? They cut it down.

"They were always putting us down because we were different from them. They got the dates with all the hot girls and they got away with stuff because they were football heroes. It just wasn't fair!"

"Y-Y-You got that right. It's n-n-not fair and I'm n-n-not going to t-t-take it anymore."

"I totally understand, but what I've learned over fifty years is that none of this stuff really matters. Once you're away from here, everything changes. Oh, sure, there are always going to be jerks out there, but you have all of your life to make a difference and do whatever it is that you want to do. But if you do this today, you'll never get that chance."

"B-B-But they have to pay!"

"Not like this,"

I turned to the kid that was on his knees shaking like a leaf. I noticed that the front of his pants were wet.

"I was in the store that day when you were

embarrassing Warren. Are you beginning to see the bigger picture here?"

He nodded his head.

"Is there anything you'd like to say to Warren?"

He nodded. "I'm so sorry, man. I just never thought --- I never realized how much we were hurting you. Please don't ---!"

I could see that Warren was wavering. He looked around the room at the horrified faces of his classmates.

"Let's end this, Warren. If you pull that trigger, your life will be over in an instant, but if you give me the gun, we can get you some help. Don't let a tragedy be the last thing your classmates remember about you. Let's work through this so that you can come back fifty years from now and show everyone what you've accomplished."

A girl's small voice spoke from the back of the room.

"Warren, we're so sorry. You've taught all of us a lesson. We don't want to see you hurt."

I saw his shoulders slump and his arm drop.

I put my arm around him and took the gun from his shaking hand.

At that moment, the door burst open and the First Response Team flooded the room.

"Don't hurt him. He's a good kid," I said as they led Warren away.

I turned and was face to face with Commander Crowder.

"Officer Williams, you disobeyed a direct order. I don't know whether you're a hero or a fool --- maybe both. Either way, your Captain will be hearing about this in my report."

He turned and stomped away.

I was sure that the Captain would be thrilled.

I was riding an adrenalin high as I met my classmates coming out of the hall bathrooms.

Maggie rushed to my side.

"Walt, are you all right?"

"I'm fine."

Eddie Delaney was right behind her.

"Well, well, looks like little Walt is quite the hero!"

Suddenly, all of the frustration that I had bottled up during those high school years boiled to the surface. I spun his pudgy torso around, grabbed the back of his under shorts and lifted until he was on his tiptoes.

"That's for Warren and all of us just like him, you asshole!"

I took Maggie by the arm.

"Let's get out of here!"

CHAPTER 15

After the tour, we stopped for a sandwich and by the time we arrived at the apartment, I had a few hours to practice my Elvis routine. I had to be back to the Polk football stadium at six o'clock to meet the other unfortunate souls that were members of the Powder Puff Cheerleading Squad.

Wanda and her reunion committee had turned the Friday night football game into a real three-ring circus.

After the Polk High varsity squad takes the field, Eddie Delaney and the other surviving members of the football team from my class will be introduced along with the girls that played in the infamous Powder Puff Game. My companions and I will join the varsity cheerleaders to whip the fans in the stadium into a football feeding frenzy.

What could possibly go wrong with all of that?

It had been a couple of years since I did my Elvis routine, but I had practiced it so much at that time, it had been hardwired into my brain, kind of like my ballroom dance steps with Maggie. It may be months between our dancing nights out, but when the music starts, the muscle memory takes over and the intricate steps of the cha-cha and rumba are always there.

I had decided to use the same set that I had used in my undercover performance at the Sprint Center. The music was already burned on a disk and I really didn't have the time to work up anything new.

I always get goose bumps when I hear *Also Sprach Zarathustra*, the theme from the movie *2001 A Space Odyssey*, which Elvis used to open his live performances in his later years.

I can see Elvis backstage, a superstar and veteran performer, anxiously awaiting the moment that he would stride onstage to a standing ovation of his fans.

I open with that, which leads right into *Si Si Rider*. I follow that rousing number with the mellower *Blue Hawaii*. That is the number where I will initiate Ox's plan to smoke out the New Theatre Restaurant shooter. The set ends with *Jailhouse Rock* and *Heartbreak Hotel*.

Fortunately, I was able to rent the same white jumpsuit that I had used earlier. I had purchased the wig, because thankfully, they don't rent those out. I dug around in the closet and found it wadded up with the elf suit that I had used in another undercover gig.

To my dismay, it looked more like a rat's nest than Elvis' famous pompadour. I must have tucked it away before all the perspiration had dried, giving it the distinct odor of old gym socks. Maggie came to the rescue with a can of Febreze, a brush and some hairspray.

Maggie had also sewn Ox's little surprise into the lining of one of the red silk scarves that I would be draping around the necks of my adoring fans while crooning *Blue Hawaii.*

After running through the set several times and grabbing a quick bite to eat, I headed to the locker room of the Polk High School football stadium to meet up with Don, Loren, Gary and Kenny, my cohorts in the Powder Puff Cheering Squad.

Eddie Delaney and five other jocks were already there. They had been given varsity pads and uniforms to wear when they took the field with the football squad. They were checking out the pads, helmets and other accoutrements that the gridiron gladiators wear.

Our squad had also been given uniforms --- Pep Club sweaters that had obviously belonged to some of the more robust members. If we had been making a movie, the title would probably have been *Grumpy Old Men in Tights*.

Naturally, Eddie couldn't resist the opportunity to give his usual ration of grief to the less athletically inclined.

"Hey! It's the Powder Puff girls --- ooops --- I mean boys. Cheer pretty for us tonight!"

He did a high-five with his buddy, Duane, and the six of them had a good laugh.

"We'd better get going," Eddie said, looking at his watch. He turned to us with a smirk, "The newspaper wants to interview the members of our class football team --- you know, the real heroes, not the Poop Club, so hold down the fort. We'll be back to dress out in about fifteen minutes."

When he passed by me, he whispered, “I’ll get you for that wedgie this morning.”

Kenny, who had been on the school tour, overheard his comment. “You got the jerk really well. You should have seen him waddling into the men’s room to extract his shorts from his crack.”

Don just shook his head. “Some things just don’t change --- even after fifty years!”

I was still burning from my morning’s experience with Warren. The poor guy had been driven over the edge by insensitive oafs like Eddie Delaney. Fortunately, my friends and I had enough positive things going for us in our lives that we were able to ignore their crap and get on with our lives, but others, not so fortunate, had been pushed to unspeakable acts by the bullying of these Neanderthals.

An unspeakable act of my own popped into my mind. “How would you guys like to even the score?”

“I’ve been waiting fifty years,” Loren replied. “What’s the plan?”

I had noticed a medicine cabinet on the wall. I opened it and looked over the various bottles and jars until I spotted what I was looking for, Analgesic Balm.

Any athlete that has ever had a sore or strained muscle is well acquainted with the greasy salve, that when applied to the aching muscle, immediately generates intense heat that penetrates deep into the muscle tissue. Once the initial scalding sensation subsides, relief is usually forthcoming, but the first jolt can be quite a shocker.

I held up the jar. "Jock straps, anyone?"

I passed the jar around and we each massaged a liberal coating of the fiery balm into the nut sack of our nemesis' jock straps.

We had just finished, when our guys and the varsity squad burst into the locker room following their interview.

It was close to game time, so they wasted no time donning their football apparel.

The coach entered, gave a brief pep talk and the team headed for the field.

The varsity cheerleaders were already there, holding a big paper banner on which was emblazoned, 'Polk High Wildcats'.

The team, lead by the captain, burst through the banner followed by Eddie and his cronies. The Powder Puff Girls from my class came next, and we, of course, were last.

Everyone lined up on the sidelines facing a packed stadium of fans that were chanting, "POLECATS! POLECATS! POLECATS!"

The announcers voice came over the intercom.

"Ladies and gentlemen. Before our National Anthem and the start of our game, I'd like to introduce some special guests we have with us tonight."

I noticed that Eddie and his buddies were having a difficult time standing still. They were fidgeting around, hopping up and down and giving one another questioning looks.

The announcer continued, "The fiftieth reunion of the 1962 graduating class of Polk High School is tomorrow evening and we are honored to have with us tonight, members of the varsity squad from 1962. I'd like to introduce them now."

Before he could announce the first name, Eddie grabbed his crotch, screamed and made a beeline for the locker room followed by his five buddies, each clutching their privates.

The timing couldn't have been more perfect.

This certainly wasn't in the announcer's script, but after a brief pause, he bravely continued. "Also with us are the members of the Girl's Powder Puff Team and their cheerleaders. Please take a bow."

We all did our thing and the game got underway.

The varsity cheerleaders, all young, lithe and nimble, led the stadium with intricate lifts, tumbles and flips.

The Powder Puff girls had been given honorary places on the bench. After a few impressive cheers by the varsity girls, one of our gals bellowed. "POWDER PUFF! POWDER PUFF! POWDER PUFF!" **

See photo, page # 231

The leader of the varsity girls motioned for us to take the field.

I looked at my friends. "You guys ready for this?"

"No fool like an old fool," Don replied. "Let's do this!"

We fell in line and barked out our basic cheer.

Two bits, four bits, six bits a dollar.
All for the Polecats, stand up and holler!

Immediately, the crowd jumped to their feet, waving their arms and screaming.

Buoyed by our success, Loren whispered, "Let's do the knees."

"I don't know if we should."

"So what are they going to do, suspend us?"

He had a point.

We lined up again.

Rah, rah ree
Kick 'em in the knee.
Rah, rah, rass
Kick 'em in the other knee!

I looked into the stands. As promised, Ox was there, laughing his ass off. Maggie was sitting beside him. Her head was bowed and she was slumped down, covering her eyes. I think she was trying to be inconspicuous, hoping no one would remember that the old guy making a fool of himself on the field was her husband.

After the last cheer, the Pep Club sponsor had given us a dirty look. I figured we were probably through cheering when one of the gals on the bench yelled, "DO NORFOLK!"

I shook my head, but the rest of the girls joined in, "DO NORFOLK!"

I looked at the guys and they just shrugged a 'why not', so we lined up again.

We're from Norfolk, couldn't be prouder.
If you can't hear us now, we'll yell a little louder.
We don't smoke!
We don't drink!
Nooooooor Folk!

As soon as the cheer was over, I saw the Pep Club sponsor heading our way. She wasn't a happy camper.

At that same moment, Eddie and the bruisers were coming back on the field from the locker room. I could see the fire in their eyes from fifty feet away.

"Looks like it might be time to wrap this up," I said.

"Good thinking," Don replied.

"Exit, stage left?" Kenny suggested.

We all nodded and took off for the parking lot with six angry giants waddling after us, shaking their fists.

I turned out to be a pretty good evening after

all.

Our team had won the game and the Powder Puff Cheerleaders had struck a blow for nerds everywhere!

CHAPTER 16

At last the big day had arrived.

I had spent the afternoon running through my program and limbering up the old bones for the hip swivels and gyrations that I had copied from the King.

After the obligatory shower, shave and shampoo, I packed up my jumpsuit, wig and music disk and we headed to the ball.

Maggie was gorgeous, as usual, and at her insistence, I donned my one suit and tie that I normally only wear to weddings and funerals. I made an exception just for her.

The reunion was to be held in the ballroom of one of the fancy hotels.

The decorating committee, minus the old guy that was practicing Elvis, had spent most of the day blowing up balloons and stringing crepe paper.

After we had registered, we entered the ballroom and I had to say that I was impressed. Every table was set with a linen cloth and napkins and a fall floral bouquet. Helium filled balloons and crepe paper were everywhere. It was like we had stepped back in time fifty years to our senior prom.

In one corner, our bales of straw and corn stalks helped promote the fall motif. The committee had placed little battery-operated candles in our jack-o-lanterns and the glow through the grotesque faces carved by my inebriated friends was actually quite appropriate. I made a mental note to take some photos to share with the gang.

Across the room, I spotted Ox and Judy dressed in hotel attire.

Detective Blaylock had hit a brick wall in the New Theatre Restaurant shooting. The only person with any possible motive was Archie Sanders and he was sitting at my table when the shot was fired. Martha Woodstock was conveniently missing from her table, but there was no concrete evidence to link her to the shooting.

Ox had speculated that Archie could have been involved and that he was working in concert with Martha, or, Martha might have been acting on her own to get into Archie's good graces. He had come up with a plan that might give us the answers and the Captain had signed off on it.

Ox was at the party undercover as a bus boy and Judy as a server.

Maggie had sewn a tiny microphone into the seam of one of the scarves that Elvis would be draping around adoring necks. My job was to make sure that Martha got the right one. Ox, Judy and I would be wearing tiny ear buds to pick up any conversation that might have a bearing on our case.

I sauntered over and Ox slipped the ear bud

into my hand. We were set to go.

I spotted Don, Kenny and their wives at a nearby table and I steered Maggie in that direction.

After introductions had been made, I glanced around the room. Eddie Delaney and his jock buddies were congregated at two tables side by side, the cheerleaders were huddled together at another and I had unconsciously drifted to the table occupied by my geek buddies.

It was quite a revelation about human nature. Fifty years had passed, we had become wrinkled and frail, but the relationships that we had forged at Polk High were as strong as ever. Although the packaging had aged and possibly mellowed, the underlying personalities had remained much the same. Bodies certainly change, but people rarely do.

Suddenly, heads began to swivel. Martha Woodstock had just walked in the door.

She was wearing a low-cut sequiny sheath that most definitely accented her silicone-enhanced bosom. I noticed that several of the women glanced at their own breasts that had obviously migrated in a southward direction over the years. Not Martha's.

Her dress had a saucy slit up the side that revealed a well-toned leg and her pouty lips were probably filled with Botox.

Martha looked twenty years younger than any other woman in the ballroom.

The perfect social butterfly, she flitted from group to group, smiling, shaking hands and giving hugs. You could see the wives rolling their eyes at the same time that their husband's eyes were focused on her ample cleavage.

She finally got around to our table.

"Walter, so nice to see you again." She glanced at Maggie. "You too, of course. Have you seen Archie?"

"No, but I'm sure he'll be here. He said he would."

"Well, I certainly hope so," she said flitting off to the next table.

I felt Maggie's fingernails biting into my thigh and I quickly averted my eyes.

Wanda Pringle stepped up to the microphone and announced that it was time to begin and that everyone should take their seats.

Dutifully, everyone returned to the chairs where they had deposited personal items to reserve their places.

Martha had found an empty seat at one of the jock's tables. At the last moment, Archie Sanders walked in the door and he took the only remaining empty chair next to Irma Turnbull.

The look on Martha's face told me that she wasn't a happy camper.

I was surprised that Wanda called on John Clevenger to offer the opening prayer. My recollection of John was that he was the first of my classmates to offer me a can of booze from a six-pack he had swiped from his older brother. I would never have guessed that John would become the pastor of a Presbyterian Church until his retirement. Maybe people do change.

After the prayer, we were sent to the buffet line, table by table. Our table was one of the last to go. While we were waiting, Ox had been busy filling water glasses. One of the guys at my table must have been really dry. He downed his glass of water immediately and signaled to Ox.

"Bus boy. I wonder if I could get a refill?"

When Ox sauntered over to fill his glass, I held mine up. "How about some ice, bus boy?"

He leaned over and whispered, "You can kiss my ice, funny guy!"

After the meal, Wanda took the mike and launched into the part of the evening when class officers, aged class teachers and committee members were introduced. That was the cue for Maggie and I to sneak out of the room to get me dressed.

The hotel had given us a storeroom in which we could change without being seen. Only Wanda and the entertainment committee knew about Elvis' visit. It was to be a surprise for the rest of the class.

I climbed into my jumpsuit, Maggie slipped on my wig and made last minute adjustments, and the scarves were placed around my neck in the proper order. I was ready for my second undercover assignment as an Elvis impersonator.

Maggie slipped back into the room and I stood outside the big double doors listening for the first notes of the stirring anthem that opened Elvis' last shows.

Unless someone has been there, it is hard to

explain the mixture of fear, excitement, expectation and pure adrenalin that courses through your body while you're waiting for that magic moment.

The moment came and I burst through the door, welcomed by the cheers, hoots, hollers and applause of my classmates.**

The ovation was not for me, but for the idol that I was portraying. It's almost like when an American flag enters a room. The flag itself may be old, torn and tattered, but the homage that is given is not for the material of which it is made, it is for all that the flag represents. Likewise, I knew that the cheers were not for me, but for one of the greatest voices and entertainers that ever lived.

After my grand entrance, I took the stage and wiggled through *Si Si Rider*. After my opening number, I always like to add a bit of humor to my act so that folks won't think I take myself too seriously.

I opened with Elvis' classic line, "Thank you. Thank you very much. I especially want to thank you for inviting me to the annual potluck of the Shady Rest Nursing Home."

I pretended like I was getting a message from an ear bud. "What? This isn't the Shady Rest Nursing Home?"

I took a long look at the aged faces in the audience. "Are you sure?"

That brought the laughs that I was hoping for.

**See photo, page# 232

After a few more introductory remarks, I cued the DJ and the beautiful strains of *Blue Hawaii* filled the room.

I had four scarves to give and I figured Wanda Pringle deserved one for all her hard work. Wanda giggled like a schoolgirl when I placed the first scarf around her neck and kissed her cheek.**

The second one went to Gladys Finch. I was looking around the room for a third victim when I noticed my old nemesis, Eddie Delaney, sulking at his table. His wife seemed to really be into the Elvis thing, so I thought, *"Why not?"*

I put on my sexiest saunter and got down on one knee in front of Eddie's wife, just as the words, *"Come with me, while the moon is on the sea,"* filled the room. I put the scarf around her neck and gave her a big hug. You can get away with stuff like that when you're being someone else.

I could almost see the steam rising from Eddie's collar as I made my way to Martha Woodstock to deliver the last scarf.

Martha played it to the hilt. Seeing this as a golden opportunity to show off her store-bought body, she seductively swayed to the final notes as Elvis sang, *"That magic night of nights with you."* As I was walking away, she reached out and gave me a pinch on the butt. I just hoped that Maggie would remember that this was police work.

Dirty business, but somebody has to do it.

**See photo, page# 232

I finished the set with *Jailhouse Rock* and *Heartbreak Hotel* and exited the ballroom to the cheers of my classmates.**

Maggie met me in the dressing room. "Nice work, Romeo."

I wasn't sure whether she was being complimentary or sarcastic. She kept me in suspense for a moment before she broke into laughter. "That was a blast!"

I had just slipped out of my jumpsuit when Maggie grabbed my BVD's and exposed my butt cheek. "Just wanted to see if Martha left a mark." When she slapped me on the rear end, I knew everything was okay.

I was anxious to see if the microphone in the scarf was working, so I put the bud in my ear.

Martha was talking to one of the other women at her table.

"Was that Walt Williams?" the woman asked.

"Sure was," Martha replied. "I dated him a few times in high school. He was a sweet boy."

That's what every guy wants to hear. 'Sweet boy!' In the next sentence they tell you, 'How about we just be friends?'

"Well I think he has a cute butt," the woman replied.

I was glad that we hadn't given Maggie an ear bud of her own.

** See photos, page # 233

By the time we returned to the ballroom, the DJ was playing all our favorite old fifties tunes.

We rocked around the clock with Bill Haley and the Comets and gazed into each other's eyes as the Platters crooned *Only You*.

It wouldn't have been a fifties dance without the *Twist* and *The Stroll* and pretty much everyone was having a great time.

I kept my eye on Martha, expecting her to jump on Archie like a duck on a June bug, but Archie's attention seemed to be on his tablemate, Irma Turnbull. Every time another song started, Archie was dancing with Irma or some guy, hoping to get lucky, had grabbed Martha and drug her to the dance floor.

I saw Martha get up and head to the ladies room. I got Maggie's attention and suggested that she accompany her and see what she could drag out of her.

I signaled Ox and Judy and we both listened intently.

"Hi, Martha," Maggie said. "Great party, don't you think?"

"Maybe for you, but not for me."

"Oh really? Why not?"

"I came here hoping to have some time with Archie, but that slut, Irma Turnbull, has had her clutches in him all evening."

Martha certainly doesn't beat around the bush.

Maggie took the lead. "Walt told me that you

and Archie dated in high school. Have you seen him much since then?"

"Unfortunately, no. He went away to school and for most of his life, he's been traveling around the country with some stage show. I was hoping that during his three months in Kansas City at the New Theatre Restaurant, that we could reconnect, but it hasn't turned out that way. I even ----."

"Even what?" Maggie asked.

"Nothing! Never mind! We'd better get back."

I thought that we almost had her.

Fifteen minutes later, the DJ announced that the next dance would be a Sadie Hawkins Dance. The girls would ask the guys.

Irma Turnbull had been in the powder room herself and returned to find Martha holding her hand out to Archie.

Archie graciously accepted and left Irma fuming at the table.

I Only Have Eyes For You by the Flamingos filled the room, and through my ear bud, I heard Martha whisper, "Remember this song, Archie. We parked by the lake and when this song came on the radio we danced in the moonlight."

"Sure I remember," he replied. "Those were good times."

"I've missed you, Archie. I've been waiting for you, you know."

"Waiting? Waiting for what?"

"For us to be together again, silly. I knew ---

after the prom --- when we --- you know --- I just knew we were meant to be together. You were my first."

"Look, Martha, I hope you didn't get the wrong idea. That was a long time ago. We were just kids fooling around. It didn't mean anything."

Ohh Ohh! That wasn't the message that Martha had been waiting all these years to hear.

"Didn't mean anything! You asshole! It meant everything to me!"

"I'm so sorry, but you need to move on."

"Move on? You want me to move on? After all that I've done for you?"

"What?" Archie asked bewildered. "What have you done for me?"

"You bastard! I shot that actor so you could get the lead and now you're dumping me like yesterday's garbage!"

"You did what?"

That was all that we needed.

I signaled to Ox and made my way to the dance floor.

I tapped Archie on the shoulder. "May I cut in?"

"Get lost, Walter!" Martha said. "We're busy here."

"Sorry, Martha, can't do it this time," I said, showing her my badge.

Archie backed away and I started dancing with Martha.

"You heard, didn't you?" she asked.

"Yeah, we did. Microphone in the scarf."

"So what happens now?"

"It's armed criminal action, Martha. I'm afraid we'll have to take you downtown --- in handcuffs, unfortunately. We can either do it here on the dance floor in front of your classmates or we can waltz over to that young lady by the door and she can do it out in the hall. Your choice."

Martha looked around the ballroom. "You always were a gentleman, Walter. Thank you. Let's dance."

I twirled her toward the door and handed her off to Judy.

As Judy was leading her away, Martha turned, "Looks like I made some wrong choices fifty years ago. I'm so sorry."

I nodded, but I wasn't sorry. If she hadn't dumped me fifty years ago, I might not be with Maggie today, and that's what mattered the most.

When I returned, the DJ was playing Ivory Joe Hunter's, *Since I Met You Baby, I'm A Happy Man.*

I grabbed Maggie and held her close.

"Any regrets?" she whispered in my ear as we swayed together on the dance floor.

"Not a one!"

At the stroke of midnight, Wanda declared that the fiftieth class reunion of Polk High School was officially at an end.

Classmates hugged and said, what for many, would be last goodbyes.

I was about to join the other members of the decorating committee whose task was to tear down all of the crepe paper and pop the balloons, when I felt a tap on my shoulder.

It was Elana Gonzales. Elana was one of those classmates that you always knew was there, but somehow just never connected with --- different classes, different circle of friends.

"Hi, Elana."

"Hi, Walt. I really enjoyed your performance tonight. Who would have guessed fifty years ago that you would be doing Elvis impersonations?"

"Certainly not me. What can I do for you?"

She hesitated, but forged ahead. "I understand that you are a police officer."

I nodded.

"It's my granddaughter, Sylvia. She has a friend that is in deep trouble. She fears for her life, but she is afraid to go to the police. I thought maybe you could help."

I started putting two and two together --- a young Latino girl in deep trouble.

"Elana, does the name Hector Corazon mean anything to you?"

She looked surprised. "So you know?"

"I know what that animal has been doing with young Latino girls. Is that what Sylvia's friend is mixed up in?"

She nodded.

"Let's meet tomorrow --- one o'clock at Mel's Diner on Broadway. Bring Sylvia. Can you do that?"

"We'll be there. Thank you, Walt."

I certainly never figured that my class reunion would end with the arrest of one of my classmates and a lead to the drug cartel that had been stumping the department for months.

Lady Justice certainly works in mysterious ways.

CHAPTER 17

Ox and I actually arrived at Mel's Diner at noon. We figured that since we were already going to be there, we might as well enjoy one of Mel's high-calorie, fat-laden meals.

We had just polished off big pieces of lemon cream pie when Elana and her granddaughter slipped into the booth.

Elana gave Ox a questioning look. "Hi Walt. Just wondering why you brought the bus boy to our meeting."

It was a natural mistake. Ox had probably filled her water glass.

"Hi Elana. Ox is my partner. He was at the reunion on special assignment. It's a long story."

I saw no reason to spread the news about Martha's arrest. The Polk High rumor mill would be buzzing soon enough.

"So this must be Sylvia," I said, turning to the pretty young lady across the booth.

"Hello, Mr. Williams," she replied, shyly.

"You can call me Walt, and this big guy is Ox. How can we help you?"

"It's my friend, Sophia. Sophia Sanchez. She has gotten involved with some very bad men and she's afraid for her life."

"Hector Corazon?" I asked.

She nodded. "He has been talking to many young women in our community. With the economy like it is, money has been tight and he has been offering a lot of it to the girls that join him."

"Have you been approached?"

"Yes, a month ago --- at the same time as Sophia. I told Granny about it and she said to stay far away from those men."

"You have a very wise grandmother. I'm guessing that Sophia wasn't as fortunate."

"No, she wasn't. Her family was deep in debt and she saw this as an opportunity to help. In the beginning, she just didn't realize the danger."

"But now she does? What changed her mind?"

"Another friend of ours signed up with Corazon just before her and now our friend has gone missing. Sophia is afraid the same thing will happen to her."

"That friend wouldn't be Rosalina Torres, would it?" Ox asked.

Sylvia was shocked. "You know of Rosalina?"

Ox and I exchanged glances. We really didn't want to tell the girl that her friend was most likely dead.

"We knew that she was coming back to Kansas City after her operation, but we haven't been able to locate her."

"I think I understand," she said, gravely.

"Why have you come to us now?" Ox asked.

"I received a text from Sophia yesterday. She has had the operation and will be returning to Kansas City tomorrow to have the implants removed. She is frightened and doesn't want to disappear like Rosalina."

"Do you know how she is returning to Kansas City --- what airline?"

"No, all the text said was that she would be returning --- but her last words were, 'Please help me!'"

"You've done the right thing coming to us." With as much conviction as I could muster, I said, "Try not to worry. We'll get on top of this and bring your friend home safe. Do you, by any chance, have a photo of Sophia?"

Sylvia nodded and pulled her cell phone out of her purse.

"I took this just before she left."

"Perfect!" I said, and we transferred the photo to my phone.

As they were leaving, Elana took my hand. "Thank you, Walt. I knew I could count on you."

With the way that we had let poor Rosalina Torres slip through our fingers, I wasn't nearly as confident of our success. I just hoped that we would do a better job this time.

"What's so important that you have to drag me away from my family on a Sunday?" the Captain asked as we met in his office. "Oh, by the way, Detective Blaylock said to give you boys a pat on the back for the New Theatre arrest. Nice work."

"Thanks," Ox replied. "Sorry to mess up your day, but we have some intel on Hector Corazon's operation that we think you'll want to hear."

In the next fifteen minutes, we brought the Captain up to speed on our visit with Elana and Sylvia."

"Looks like we're going to have to mess up Rocky Winkler's weekend as well," the Captain said. "We don't want to screw up this opportunity."

The rest of the afternoon was spent coordinating with the Drug Enforcement Unit. When Corazon's men pick up Sophia Sanchez at the airport, we want to be there to tail them to their base of operation and end this thing once and for all.

Ernie and Father O'Brian had spent hours sitting behind the dumpster in the old Buick, watching the warehouse and hoping for another lead to pass on to the police, but since that first day, traffic in and out of the building had been sparse, certainly nothing to warrant police involvement.

Ernie had just poured a cup of coffee in Father O'Brian's kitchen. "Shall we give it another day, Father?"

"Do you have something more pressing?" Paddy replied, sarcastically.

"No, I guess I don't, but I can't go until later. I have an early appointment with Doc Johnson. He's upping the dosage of my pain medicine. Between the damned cancer and sitting cramped up in that car for hours, I'm hurting pretty bad."

"Maybe you could slip me a couple of whatever the Doc gives you," Paddy said. "I've been pretty uncomfortable myself."

Just then the phone rang.

"Patrick O'Brian here."

"Father O'Brian. This is Marlena Sanchez."

"Senora Sanchez! How nice to hear from you. What can I do for you?"

"It's my daughter, Sophia. She needs help and I'm afraid to go to the police. I didn't know where else to turn, so I'm calling you. She always trusted you."

Paddy punched the speakerphone button so that Ernie could hear the conversation.

"Is this about Hector Corazon?"

"How did you know?"

"I heard about Rosalina Torres. I know what Corazon is doing with our girls. How can I help?"

"Sophia is coming back to Kansas City this afternoon. That is all I know. If Corazon thinks that I have talked to the police, Sophia will not be safe and neither will the rest of my family."

"You are right, Marlena. Don't talk to anyone

else. I will handle this. We'll get Sophia back for you."

“Thank you, Father. I was praying that you could help."

Paddy hung up the phone and turned to his friend. “This is the break we've been looking for. When Sophia Sanchez steps out of that van, we'll be there and we'll have enough proof to bring the cops running. Go get your drugs and let's get out of here!"

We had missed Rosalina Torres because we had mistakenly assumed that she would be coming on a direct flight from Mexico and would be passing through customs. Corazon had fooled us when he sent her to Denver to pass through customs and spend the night. We hadn't bothered to check on the dozens of other flights coming from cities all across the country.

Winkler wasn't about to make the same mistake again.

He had commandeered every available officer and posted a man at every gate in the airport. The name Sophia Sanchez was not listed on any incoming flight, but given Corazon's slippery tactics, she could have been booked under another name. Every officer had the photo of Sophia that Sylvia had given us.

The plan was the same as before. Sophia would be met at the gate by one of Corazon's men.

The two of them would be tailed to the location where the drugs were to be surgically removed. Once that location was known, Winkler would hit the building with everything he had.

Unmarked cars were located at every terminal and airport exit to tail Sophia when she exited the building.

Ox and I were in one of the unmarked cars.

Since we had no idea what flight she might be on, we started our surveillance at five in the morning, with the first flight to arrive in Kansas City.

Surveillance is a boring, mind-numbing job at best. We had hoped that Sophia would be on an early flight, but, of course, that didn't happen. Every time a plane landed, we waited expectantly for the message that Sophia had been spotted, but by one in the afternoon, there had been no sign of her.

After eight hours sitting in the car, our butts were numb and there was the possibility that we might be there another ten hours until the last flight of the day had landed.

We had taken turns running to the john and to Starbucks, but even filled with Espresso Grande, we were having a hard time staying alert.

I had just polished off my fourth Grande when my cell phone rang.

"Walter?"

"Yes."

"This is Elana Gonzales. Where are you?"

"We're at the airport. We have the place staked out, watching for Sophia."

"Then you're in the wrong place!"

"What!"

"Sylvia just received a text from Sophia. At two o'clock, she'll be arriving at the Greyhound Bus Terminal from Little Rock, Arkansas."

"Thanks, Elana. We gotta go!"

I looked at my watch. "Let's hit it, partner. We've got less than an hour to get to the Greyhound Bus Terminal. Corazon screwed us again!"

Ox peeled away from the terminal and I got on the horn to report the bad news that all of Rocky Winkler's resources were in the wrong place.

By the time we got away from the terminal and made the long drive from KCI to the Greyhound Terminal at Eleventh and Troost, it was five minutes after two.

"There," Ox said, pointing to a black SUV. "Isn't that Sophia?"

I just had time to get a glimpse of her before she was shoved into the van.

"That's her, all right. I wonder if they'll be heading to the City Market?"

Ox fell into traffic behind the van that headed west on Twelfth Street.

I radioed the fact that we had eyes on Sophia and that they were headed west on Twelfth.

I was surprised when the van zipped through the Walnut Street intersection and continued west.

"Not going to the City market," Ox observed. "Must have found a new spot."

When the van entered the Twelfth Street

Viaduct, we knew that their destination was most likely the West Bottoms.

"Lots of old warehouses down there," Ox said, "but which one?"

I radioed our position to Rocky Winkler.

"We're five minutes behind you," he replied. "Don't lose them!"

The van turned onto Mulberry and headed north, then it took a left on Eighth Street, and finally turned into a warehouse parking lot on Hickory.

I radioed the location to Winkler.

We pulled to the curb and watched as the driver and another man dragged Sophia out of the van.

Suddenly, the radio exploded.

"SHIT!"

"Sergeant Winkler. What's happening?"

"Train! It's blocking the intersection. We can't get to you until it passes! You're on your own until we can get there!"

We looked, and the two goons were pushing Sophia toward the door to the warehouse.

"It wasn't supposed to go down like this!" I said. "Rocky was supposed to hit the place before they got Sophia inside. If they get her in there and then realize we're coming, they'll just butcher the poor girl to get the drugs. We have to do something!"

I put a red light on the top of the unmarked car and Ox hit the accelerator.

The sound of the tires squealing on the pavement got the attention of Sophia's captors. One of them shoved her behind the van and the other one drew an automatic pistol and aimed it at our oncoming car.

The first hail of bullets hit the grille and headlights.

Ox spun the car sideways and we scrambled behind it just as the second wave smashed into the door panel.

We tried to return fire, but the rounds from the automatic pistol kept us pinned down.

Somehow, the bad guys always manage to have better guns than the cops!

There was a brief pause and I figured the guy was putting a new clip into the pistol. I peered over the hood and what I saw made my blood run cold. The first man had emerged from behind the van and he was carrying a grenade launcher!

Ernie and Father O'Brian had been sitting behind the dumpster since eleven o'clock.

Each had taken one of Doc Johnson's pain pills, but the long wait was beginning to take its toll.

Ernie looked at his watch.

"Two-thirty. Do you think Mrs. Sanchez got it wrong?"

Just then, a black SUV pulled into the parking lot followed by an old Ford.

"Maybe this is it!" Paddy said.

They watched as the two men climbed out of the van.

"There she is!" Paddy exclaimed. That's her. Let's call the cops."

Before he could pick up the phone, the old Ford shot forward with a red light flashing on top.

"That ***is*** the cops!" Paddy said. "Halleluiah!"

Their jubilation turned to concern when one of the thugs pulled an automatic pistol and fired at the oncoming vehicle.

The Ford skidded to a halt and two men took shelter behind it.

"That's ***our*** cops!" Ernie said. "The old guy and the big one. The ones we wrote to."

They watched as the rounds from the automatic pistol slammed into the car.

"They're pinned down," Paddy said. "Where's their back up?"

Just then they heard the whistle of a train.

"Jesus, Paddy! Remember when we tailed those guys the first day and got stuck behind a train?"

Paddy nodded.

"Well that's what's happened to their backup!"

There was a brief moment when the firing ceased. They saw the shooter slamming another clip in his pistol. Then the second man emerged from behind the van.

"Oh, my God!" Ernie exclaimed.

"What? What is it?"

"That guy has a grenade launcher. I saw a

documentary about them on PBS. One of those things can take out a tank. Those guys don't stand a chance. That old Ford will be toast and so will the cops."

Father O'Brian was silent for a moment.

"Ernie, do you remember when Frank was alive, we called ourselves the Three Amigos?"

Ernie nodded.

"Frank gave his life to save ours and we're just two amigos now. What would you say about changing movies?"

"To what?"

"*Butch Cassidy and The Sundance Kid.*"

"As I recall that didn't turn out too well for Butch and Sundance."

"Think about it, Ernie. Before long we're both going to be bedridden. They're going to be sticking catheters up our dicks and pumping us full of morphine. Is that really the way you want to go out? We have a chance here to make our lives count for something. What do you say?"

He thought about it for just a moment. "Okay Amigo. Let's do this!"

Ernie fired up the old Buick and stepped on the gas, the two friends clasped their hands together for the last time and headed straight for the man holding the grenade launcher.

The last time I had seen one of those fearsome weapons, I was on a dock on the Missouri River. I managed to jump into the river just as the grenade hit the dock. There was nothing left of the thing but splinters.

"Ox, we have a problem!"

Ox peeked over the hood and saw the launcher.

"Crap! We're sitting ducks here!"

"Think we can outrun it?"

"Not a chance!"

We were considering our limited options when we heard a car engine and squealing tires.

We saw an old Buick emerge from behind a dumpster and head directly toward the grenade launcher.

"Isn't that Ernie Harding's car?" Ox asked.

"Sure is --- and Father O'Brian's with him. What are those crazy old coots doing?"

We watched in horror as the grenade launcher turned from us to the oncoming car. The projectile hit the old Buick and it exploded into a million pieces between the van and us.

"This is our chance," Ox said. "They can't see us through the smoke and fire. Let's go!"

The train must have passed, and as we sprinted toward the remains of the smoking car, I heard the sirens of Rocky Winkler's Task Force.

The explosion had stunned the man with the grenade launcher. Ox pounced on him and was cuffing his hands when the goon with the automatic pistol emerged from behind the van.

I fired my weapon before he could react and he fell to the ground.

During the melee, Hector Corazon had come from the warehouse and grabbed Sophia. By the time we had subdued his henchmen, he was dragging her back inside.

"Let's go! We have to get to him before he can hurt her."

We sprinted to the warehouse door and peered cautiously inside. The room was dark, but on the other side, a light shone through a partially closed door.

We made our way toward the light and peered in.

Corazon was standing behind Sophia with a gun to her head.

This was their new operating room. There was a gurney and a small table filled with operating instruments.

Ox pushed the door open and we stepped inside.

"Don't come any closer or I'll kill her!" Corazon said, menacingly.

"It's over, Hector," I said. "Didn't you hear those sirens? There's no way out of here for you."

"There is if you want to save the life of this girl. My life for hers. Otherwise, she dies and I die with her."

Sophia was sobbing. "Shoot him! Just shoot him so he can't hurt any other girls! I don't care about me."

We advanced a few steps forward and Corazon stepped back.

"One more step and this girl's blood will be on your hands."

Corazon had retreated just far enough that the table full of instruments was in reach.

Sophia's hand touched the table and she instinctively looked down.

A scalpel was near her hand.

She grabbed the instrument and plunged it into Corazon's leg.

He screamed and loosened his grip just enough for her to slip away.

"Bitch!" he screamed, and pointed the gun at the shaking girl.

Ox and I fired simultaneously and the leader of the drug cartel slumped to the ground.

Hector Corazon had fallen under the very knife that he had used to disfigure his victims.

Lady Justice balances the scales in mysterious ways.

EPILOGUE

Human nature is one of the great mysteries of the universe.

Over the past few months, I had witnessed both the best and the worst of what mankind has to offer.

Intellectual debates on the subject often boil down to the battle of nature versus nurture.

Some feel that once the egg and sperm unite, that person's destiny is sealed in their DNA, while others believe that the growing embryo is a blank page who's life story is forged by the circumstances into which he is born.

I don't pretend to know the answer.

I just know there are people like Warren, who by some quirk of fate was born with a skin condition and a speech impediment.

Thankfully, not everyone that comes into the world with a handicap becomes a mass murderer. That could have happened to Warren and his story could have become the next Columbine or Sandy Hook.

Likewise, others are born with extraordinary gifts like athletic prowess. Eddie Delaney was such a man. Again, thankfully, not every gifted athlete becomes a bully. What were the influences in his life that caused him to develop that unfortunate personality trait?

An even more vexing question is what happens when the life of a man like Eddie Delaney intersects with the life of a Warren?

The result might be like the reaction that ensues when baking soda and vinegar are mixed --- a boiling cauldron that is impossible to contain.

Then there are men like Hector Corazon. What is it that hardens such a man, enabling him to murder and disfigure?

As police officers, we come in contact on a daily basis with the worst of the worst.

When that happens, we sometimes begin to lose faith in our fellow man and begin to question whether what we do is really worth risking our lives.

When such doubts creep into my mind, I often pay a visit to my old friend, Pastor Bob. He has a way of putting things in perspective.

I paid him such a visit after the shoot-out with the drug cartel.

After hearing my story, he went to his kitchen and brought back two apples. One was red, ripe and juicy and looked delicious. The other was bruised, wrinkled and most unappealing.

"People are a lot like apples," he said. "Somehow, somewhere along the way, something happens to some apples that makes them turn bad. Just because there are a few bad apples, we don't cast all apples aside. We choose the good apples and enjoy their nourishment. The good ones are worth keeping and saving.

"Yes, there are people like Hector Corazon, but there are also people like your three friends from Whispering Hills."

He picked up his worn Bible. “Let me read you something from the fifteenth chapter of John. *‘Greater love hath no man than this, that a man lay down his life for his friends.’*

“Frank Pollard was willing to lay down his life to save his two friends. Had he not done that, Father O’Brian and Ernie would not have been around to lay down their lives for you and Ox, and we wouldn’t be having this conversation today.

“I’m sure you know the story contained in this excerpt from James Foley’s famous poem, *Drop A Pebble.*

Drop a pebble in the water: just a splash, and it is gone;

But there's half-a-hundred ripples circling on and on and on.

Spreading, spreading from the center, flowing on out to the sea.

And there is no way of telling where the end is going to be.

Drop a pebble in the water: in a minute you forget,

But there's little waves a-flowing, and there's ripples circling yet,

And those little waves a-flowing to a great big wave have grown;

You've disturbed a mighty river just by dropping in a stone.

"Frank Pollard's sacrifice was the dropping of that stone. The first ripple was Ernie and Father O'Brian giving their lives for you and Ox. That allowed you to save the life of the girl. How many more lives will be touched because you and Ox are still on the job. There's a half-a-hundred ripples circling on and on and on, and there's no telling where the end is going to be. That's up to you."

As usual, Pastor Bob had helped me get my head on straight.

As I drove home, the words from St. John kept echoing in my mind.

'*Greater love hath no man than this, that a man lay down his life for his friends.*'

If these good men had been willing to lay down their lives, I wasn't about to let the ripples stop with me.

I plan on keeping those ripples flowing.

There will always be both good men and bad, and Lady Justice will always be looking for good men to help keep the scales of life in balance.

My name is Walter Williams and that's why I'm a cop!

The headstone marking the final resting place of the Beta Club tree, struck down in its infancy by hooligans. A nefarious act indeed! (Actual photo from author's yearbook.)

The author as a Powder Puff Cheerleader, Class of 1961.

The author, as a 69-year-old Elvis, making his appearance at his wife's 50th Class Reunion, October, 2012.

What woman wouldn't want to receive a scarf from the King of Rock-N-Roll?

Jailhouse Rock

Heartbreak Hotel

To see a video of the performance, go to http://www.youtube.com/watch?v=ludb2sTutSA&feature=player_detailpage#t=464s

ABOUT THE AUTHOR

Award-winning author, Robert Thornhill, began writing at the age of sixty-six, and in three short years has penned twelve novels in the Lady Justice mystery/comedy series, the seven volume Rainbow Road series of chapter books for children, a cookbook and a mini-autobiography.

The fifth, sixth, seventh and ninth novels in his Lady Justice series, *Lady Justice and the Sting, Lady Justice and Dr. Death, Lady Justice and the Vigilante* and *Lady Justice and the Candidate* won the Pinnacle Achievement Award from the National Association of Book Entrepreneurs as the best mystery novels in 2011 and 2012.

Robert holds a master's degree in psychology, but his wit and insight come from his varied occupations including thirty years as a real estate broker.

He lives with his wife, Peg, in Independence, Mo.

LADY JUSTICE TAKES A C.R.A.P.
City Retiree Action Patrol
Third Edition

This is where it all began.

See how sixty-five year old Walt Williams became a cop and started the City Retiree Action Patrol.

Meet Maggie, Willie, Mary and the Professor, Walt's sidekicks in all of the Lady Justice novels.

Laugh out loud as Walt and his band of Senior Scrappers capture the Realtor Rapist and take down the Russian Mob.

Visit Bob on the web at http://BooksByBob.com

LADY JUSTICE AND THE LOST TAPES

In *Lady Justice and the Lost Tapes*, Walt and his band of scrappy seniors continue their battle against the forces of evil.

When an entire eastside Kansas City neighborhood is terrorized by the mob, Walt must go undercover to solve the case.

Later, the amazing discovery of a previously unknown recording session of a deceased rock 'n' roll idol stuns the music industry.

Visit Bob on the web ay http://BooksByBob.com

LADY JUSTICE GETS LEI'D

In Lady Justice Gets Lei'd, Walt and Maggie plan a romantic honeymoon on the beautiful Hawaiian Islands, but ancient artifacts discovered in a cave in a dormant volcano and a surprising revelation about Maggie's past, lead our lovers into the hands of Hawaiian zealots.

Visit Bob on the web at http://BooksByBob.com

LADY JUSTICE AND THE AVENGING ANGELS

Lady Justice has unwittingly entered a religious war.

Who better to fight for her than Walt Williams?

The Avenging Angels believe that it's their job to rain fire and brimstone on Kansas City, their Sodom and Gomorrah.

In this compelling addition to the Lady Justice series, Robert Thornhill brings back all the characters readers have come to love for more hilarity and higher stakes.

You'll laugh and be on the edge of your seat until the big finish.

Don't miss *Lady Justice and the Avenging Angels!*

Visit Bob on the web at http://BooksByBob.com

LADY JUSTICE AND THE STING

BEST NEW MYSTERY NOVEL ---WINTER 2012

National Association of Book Entrepreneurs

In *Lady Justice and the Sting*, a holistic physician is murdered and Walt becomes entangled in the high-powered world of pharmaceutical giants and corrupt politicians.

Maggie, Ox Willie, Mary and all your favorite characters are back to help Walt bring the criminals to justice in the most unorthodox ways.

A dead-serious mystery with hilarious twists!

Visit Bob on the web at http://BooksByBob.com

LADY JUSTICE AND DR. DEATH

BEST NEW MYSTERY NOVEL --- FALL 2011

National Association of Book Entrepreneurs

In *Lady Justice and Dr. Death*, a series of terminally ill patients are found dead under circumstances that point to a new Dr. Death practicing euthanasia in the Kansas City area.

Walt and his entourage of scrappy seniors are dragged into the 'right-to-die-with-dignity' controversy.

The mystery provides a light-hearted look at this explosive topic and death in general.

You may see end-of-life issues in a whole new light after reading *Lady Justice and Dr. Death*!

Visit Bob on the web at http://BooksByBob.com

LADY JUSTICE AND THE VIGILANTE

BEST NEW MYSTERY NOVEL – SUMMER 2012

National Association of Book Entrepreneurs

A vigilante is stalking the streets of Kansas City administering his own brand of justice when the justice system fails.

Criminals are being executed right under the noses of the police department.

A new recruit to the City Retiree Action Patrol steps up to help Walt and Ox bring an end to his reign of terror.

But not everyone wants the vigilante stopped. His bold reprisals against the criminal element have inspired the average citizen to take up arms and defend themselves.

As the body count mounts, public opinion is split.

Is it justice or is it murder?

A moral dilemma that will leave you laughing and weeping!

Visit Bob on the web at http://BooksByBob.com

LADY JUSTICE AND THE WATCHERS

Suzanne Collins wrote *The Hunger Games*, Aldous Huxley wrote *Brave New World* and George Orwell wrote *1984*.

All three novels were about dystopian societies of the future.

In *Lady Justice and the Watchers*, Walt sees the world we live in today through the eyes of a group who call themselves 'The Watchers'.

Oscar Levant said that there's a fine line between genius and insanity.

After reading *Lady Justice and the Watchers*, you may realize as Walt did that there's also a fine line separating the life of freedom that we enjoy today and the totalitarian society envisioned in these classic novels.

Quietly and without fanfare, powerful interests have instituted policies that have eroded our privacy, health and individual freedoms.

Is the dystopian society still a thing of the distant future or is it with us now disguised as a wolf in sheep's clothing?

Visit Bob on the web at http://BooksByBob.com

LADY JUSTICE AND THE CANDIDATE

BEST NEW MYSTERY NOVEL – FALL 2012

National Association of Book Entrepreneurs

Will American politics always be dominated by the two major political parties or are voters longing for an Independent candidate to challenge the establishment?
Everyone thought that the slate of candidates for the presidential election had been set until Benjamin Franklin Foster came on the scene capturing the hearts of American voters with his message of change and reform.

Powerful interests intent on preserving the status quo with their bought-and-paid-for politicians were determined to take Ben Foster out of the race.

The Secret Service comes up with a quirky plan to protect the Candidate and strike a blow for Lady Justice.

Join Walt on the campaign trail for an adventure full of surprises, mystery, intrigue and laughs!

Visit Bob on the web at http://BooksByBob.com

LADY JUSTICE
AND THE
BOOK CLUB MURDERS

Members of the Midtown Book Club are found murdered.

It is just the beginning of a series of deaths that lead Walt and Ox into the twisted world of a serial killer.

In the late 1960's, the Zodiac Killer claimed to have killed 37 people and was never caught --- the perfect crime.

Oscar Roach, dreamed of being the next serial killer to commit the perfect crime.

He left a calling card with each of his victims --- a mystery novel, resting in their blood-soaked hands.

The media dubbed him 'The Librarian'.

Walt and the Kansas City Police are baffled by the cunning of this vicious killer and fear that he has indeed committed the perfect crime.

Or did he?

Walt and his wacky senior cohorts prove, once again, that life goes on in spite of the carnage around them.

The perfect blend of murder, mayhem and merriment.

Visit Bob on the web at http://BooksByBob.com

LADY JUSTICE AND THE CRUISE SHIP MURDERS

Ox and Judy are off to Alaska on a honeymoon cruise and invite Walt and Maggie to tag along.

Their peaceful plans are soon shipwrecked by the murder of two fellow passengers.

The murders appear to be linked to a century-old legend involving a cache of gold stolen from a prospector and buried by two thieves.

Their seven-ay cruise is spent hunting for the gold and eluding the modern day thieves intent on possessing it at any cost.

Another nail-biting mystery that will have you on the edge of your seat one minute and laughing out loud the next.

Visit Bob on the web at http://BooksByBob.com

WOLVES IN SHEEP'S CLOTHING

In August of 2011, I completed the fifth novel in the *Lady Justice* mystery/comedy series, *Lady Justice And The Sting*.

As I always do, I sent copies of the completed manuscript to several friends and acquaintances for their feedback and comments before sending the manuscript to the publisher.

Since the plot involved a holistic physician, I sent a copy to Dr. Edward Pearson in Florida.

Dr. Pearson loved the premise of the book and the style of writing, particularly as it related to alternative healthcare, natural products and Walt's transformation into a healthier lifestyle.

In subsequent conversations, Dr. Pearson shared that he had been looking for a book that he could share with his patients, colleagues and peers that would spread his message in a format that would capture their imagination and their hearts.

The Sting was very close to what he had been looking for and he made the suggestion that maybe we could work together to produce just the right book.

As I reflected on this idea, I realized that Walt's skirmishes with pharmaceutical companies, corrupt politicians, doctors, nurses, hospitals, bodily afflictions and a healthier lifestyle were not confined to just *The Sting*, but were scattered throughout all six of the *Lady Justice* mystery/comedy novels.

Using *The Sting* as the basis of the new book, I went through the manuscripts of the other five *Lady Justice* novels and pulled out chapters and vignettes that fleshed out the story of Walt's medical adventures.

Thus, *Wolves In Sheep's Clothing* was born.

Dr. Pearson is currently using *Wolves* in conjunction with his New Medicine Foundation to help spread the word about healthcare alternatives.

New Medicine Foundation
Dr. Edward W. Pearson, MD, ABIHM
http://newmedicinefoundation.com

RAINBOW ROAD
CHAPTER BOOKS FOR CHILDREN
AGES 5 – 10

Super Secrets of Rainbow Road

Super Powers of Rainbow Road

Hawaiian Rainbows

Patriotic Rainbows

Sports Heroes of Rainbow Road

Ghosts and Goblins of Rainbow Road

Christmas Crooks of Rainbow Road

For more information, go to http://BooksByBob.com

Made in the USA
Charleston, SC
11 December 2013